The Peripheral

Seen Not Heard

The Peripheral

Seen not Heard

Meena Mahanty Kumar

www.meenamahantykumar.com

The Peripheral

Seen Not Heard

First published in India in paperback in 2022 by Authorspress

Acknowledgements

For Baba who passed on his habit of transferring thoughts to random bits of paper and Ma who told a story like no one else.

Writing my book was a strange journey. Sometimes flowing and sometimes just lapping the shores of ideas, at times fulfilling, at times frustrating. That it finally got done I owe in huge part to some amazing people in my life.

I would like to begin by thanking my sister Nina without whose encouragement I would not have begun my writing journey. Thank you Neens for always being there for me.

My brother Sandeep and sister Maino for being my supportive rocks and getting me to 'pen my ideas' already!

My husband Somir for believing in me and for steadfastly pushing me to get it out there.

My offspring Ayus and Ishira for waiting patiently for the book to finally get written and wanting to be the first to read it. My nieces Mona, Poppy and Nikki for believing in my writing and encouraging me to publish. Thank you.

My dear friends Madhuri, Seema, Mona, Madhabi, Jaishri, Ruchi, Vandana, Gauri and Ipsita for keeping me grounded, encouraging me through my journey and being my family.

My friend and soulmate Upala for being my reader, for helping me look for publishers, for driving me, scolding me and for being my critic.

Dear friend Rupa Parthasarathy for being my ideas girl, for helping with my surveys and for holding my hand when I felt like giving up on the publishing journey.

My friends and support team of Shipra, Mansi and Preeti for their love and for helping me in so many ways to make my book a success.

The many real-life Kinnars who have been my source of inspiration and research, whose lives on the periphery have deeply impacted my sense of everything that is wrong.

Most of all I thank the unknown Kinnar who has been the one to make me think, feel horrified and ashamed for the way we treat people who are 'different'.

Meena Mahanty Kumar

Contents

CHAPTER 1

The Book that Started it All

Rene froze in her seat, her gaze transfixed. The 5.39 from Wynyard to St Leonards had been late and Rene's stilettoes were pinching her feet from hours standing scanning documents for her case. She bitterly regretted giving in to Rosa, her colleague at Stamford and Barnes in Sydney, who thought that block heeled, sensible shoes did *not* say successful solicitor. She found a seat and slipped off her shoes, frowning at the flaring redness of her feet. Her head still buzzed with the hum of the scanner and all she wanted to do was to put her feet up and close her eyes. Running her hand on the soft blue fabric on the seat, she stretched out, sighing almost sensuously. Rene touched her face to move a willfully wavy strand of her dark, shoulder length hair to glance around the carriage. A friendly smile curved her full lips when she caught one of the passengers staring at her. Most of the travelers in the carriage were asleep or reading after a long day. As she closed her eyes, her surroundings blurred and blunted and her tired shoulders relaxed.

'Excuse me,' said a woman softly and Rene moved to make way for her. She started, her heart thudding. There was something about the title of the book that the woman was holding. Rene leaned forward, a perplexed frown furrowing her forehead. She was hypnotized. Hypnotized by the bright orange cover of the book. Her eyes bored into the cover, looking for answers. *Why am I so fixated with this word? I have no idea what it means.* The rhythmic motion of the wheels seemed to thump with the pounding of her heart.

In between dozing and waking up at stops as the train moved on its usual route, Rene glanced at the book once again and looked the title – *The Hijras*. A strange sense of deja vu hit her. Something about that name and that vision brought on the same sort of dread that her childhood nightmares had done, a familiar sense of staring at a secret door in front of her, a door she dared not open. And just like in her nightmares, she did not know why she should sense this dread. Only, this time, the feeling did not leave her as it had done after she woke up.

What the hell is happening to me?

Lulled by the motion of the train, Rene fell into an uneasy sleep, and some five minutes later, woke up trembling, sweat beading her temples. Words she did not recognize tumbled out her lips as she woke and she heard herself muttering the word *hijra* multiple times until she forced herself to stop. As the last traces of sleep left her, she was locked in the memory of her nightmare. Of a little girl in a small, oddly shaped blue car, parked in front of what seemed to be a slum dwelling. The car had no boot, simply a flat, sloping back. There was a woman at the wheel. She was wearing a pale yellow saree and her back was towards the little girl. Suddenly that vision collided with the image of *that* title, of *that* book, The Hijras.

Rene gazed unseeingly at the passengers alighting at St Leonards. Her hands would not stop shaking despite the warm summer air. She felt a strange sense of foreboding throughout her long walk from the station to her home in the high-rise apartments near Artarmon.

I haven't had a nightmare in years! Not since mum, dad and I moved to Australia. I was, what, about eight years old? No, that's not exactly right. They had plagued me for at least two years after we had migrated, she remembered. After which they had slowly faded away, occurring infrequently. She certainly did not remember having any recurrence in the last seven or eight years.

And why on earth was she muttering that strange word, *hijra?* She did not even *know* what it meant. And yet she had the weirdest feeling that she ought to know! Where *had* she heard it?

She could not shake off her unease even while cooking her dinner, trying hard to recall where she could have heard that word.

Rene's head began to ache with the strain, and snuggling into her lilac jacquard quilt she tried to sleep. Sleep, though, eluded her. After turning on her side a few times, she gave up the effort. It was summer, and the sky was already lightening. After a quick wash, she made her way to the kitchen and switched on the kettle. Absently putting the coffee in the plunger, she remembered it was Saturday.

Since I don't have to go to work today, I might as well go for a run, Rene decided. She brushed aside the few letters and papers from the black and white Caesar stone bench top and settled down to her coffee and the unread *MX* newspaper from yesterday. The "Vent your Spleen" and "Overheard" and "Here's looking at you" columns that she usually read and which mostly had her in splits, could not interest her at all that morning.

As she made her way down the brick hued, carpeted stairs leading to the foyer, the colour jogged her memory and she remembered the book that the woman sitting next to her on the train had been reading. That was where she had seen the name – *The Hijras*! But she still couldn't understand why she had been screaming that word in her dream. Her vigorous pace during her run in the park near her apartment did not help to clear her head at all.

****

Rene forgot all about the nightmare in the next few days, caught up entirely in preparing for an important case for her firm. Being a successful solicitor in a law firm in the city meant long days and her evenings found her buried under voluminous tomes in preparation for her bar exams. It took all her working hours and more and all week she ate her meals out, barely having the time to shower before hitting her bed. There was no time to even listen to her phone messages.

On Sunday, she punched the replay button on her phone. She rolled her dark brown eyes at the twenty-five messages blinking at her accusingly. Fresh from a shower, Rene perched herself on to the bench top to listen.

'What's up dude? Disappeared under the radar again, have you? That was Helen, when Rene called her back. Seema and Helen were her two closest friends and were quite familiar with her pattern of disappearing for a few days and then resurfacing.

Rene drove to Lane Cove Plaza through the busy afternoon traffic to meet them for lunch. Impatient to see her friends, she was tempted to honk at the red Ute spewing black smoke in front of her. *Should I tell them about my nightmare on the train?* Helen and Seema knew she had been very traumatised by them as a child. They had been best friends since primary school and had remained close through high school and university. But the idea of ruining their happiness at seeing each other after such a long time with talk of nightmares, did not seem like a great plan for their meeting.

Rene's face brightened in anticipation as she switched off the ignition and, as she reached the Plaza, she greeted her two most favourite people, hugging and kissing them enthusiastically. Looking at them, Rene's mood lifted magically. The aromas drifting from their favourite Italian café distracted them and the three sat down to order their selections. Rene ordered a vegetarian spaghetti dish with haloumi cheese for herself. After they had settled down to eat, Helen leaned forward, her chin cupped in her palm, a scolding look in her eyes.

'You've been working too hard again. Look at those bags under your eyes!' She frowned. Helen's parents had moved from England before she and her brother had been born. Married to Lachlan, her university sweetheart straight after graduating, she was now the mother of a five-year-old boy, Michael. Being the only one married among them, she had assumed the role of mother hen to Seema and Rene, but had always had somewhat of a soft corner for Rene. Seema arched her brows at Rene and smiling mischievously, said,

'Mmm, must be all the late nights. With that good looking hunk at your office, Sachin, you know? That's the guy of Indian background who started in her firm a few months back.' The latter was to Helen. 'Tell me hun, did the bells jangle after all?'

'So...... out with it, Rene. What happened? Is he *the one*?' joined in Helen, all set for the interrogation.

It was a joke between them that Rene would know whether she had met the right man if bells jangled in her head. She made an exaggeratedly sad face as she said that the bells had *not*, after all, jangled. Yes, she had gone out with him a few times. For a drink and a movie. Sometimes dinner. Yes, she liked him. But nothing very momentous had happened. Certainly, no bells had rung in her head.

'You're too much of a romantic, girl. Too much of a perfectionist. You need to get a life, darling!' Seema teased gently, her kohl lined eyes disappointed because clearly, her probing had not yielded anything satisfactory.

Was she really? Rene didn't think so.

'How's *your* story going, Seema?' countered Rene, partly because she wanted to deflect the conversation away from her, and partly because she really wanted to know.

'I thought you girls would never ask,' Seema burst out and, pulling out her left hand from under the table, displayed the delicately crafted diamond ring sparkling there. 'Do you know how hard it is to eat grilled chicken using only one hand?' She fished out the bottle of champagne that she had been hiding in her voluminous bag under the table.

Glancing around, Rene grinned unapologetically as their joyous squeals and laughter drew a few frowns and acknowledging smiles from nearby tables.

'Is it Nick, the accountant at your boutique who you've been glued to for the past year?' asked Helen. Seema had studied fashion design and had opened a small boutique in Paddington only a year ago.

'Yeah, who else but my Greek God? Mum and dad have gotten over the initial shock but still lament that I couldn't find a nice Indian boy for myself. Like Sachin,' she winked at Rene, laughing. Helen pulled Seema to her feet and danced a little jig while Mike and some of the sedate patrons looked on askance. Rene smiled and looked fondly at the two, feeling pleased for her friend.

How lucky I am to have these two amazing women as my friends. You could almost reach out and touch the happiness borne out of their genuine love for each other. For a moment a pulse drummed in her temples. Rene closed her eyes, the memory of that blue car, that woman in the yellow saree, the little girl piercing into her mind when the last thing she needed was for this to intrude into her present. The cool condensation on her glass felt good against her forehead. At Helen's concerned look, Rene quickly put her drink down, smiling.

After lunch, Rene played a spot of catch with Mike, Helen's five-year-old son in the little green square of the Plaza. She loved sitting there and watching the children play. She enjoyed the village like feel of the place, the variety of cafes and the people chattering around her. As the sky darkened in the late afternoon and the birds started chirping in the trees around, a sense of peace descended on her, and she felt she could stay there forever.

But the next day was Monday, and she needed to get some ironing done and eat cooked food for a change. Feeling the need for a simple, no fuss dinner she promised Helen and Seema she would not disappear again the week after. And hugging her friends, Rene headed straight for her apartment.

'We'll hold you to that,' the other two yelled in unison, as they walked away.

Rene baked a lasagne with lamb mince, mushroom and spinach and settled down to watch one of her favourite chick flicks, 27

Dresses, while eating. As she buried deeper into the couch with an old, almost threadbare throw that had belonged to her father covering her, she fell into a dreamless sleep, her nightmare of a few days ago, all but forgotten.

****

CHAPTER 2

Who are the Hijras?

The next week passed in a haze for Rene, with work and preparation for her bar exam taking up all of her time. She felt quite pleased with the way her exam had gone and spent Saturday doing her washing and ironing and watering and fertilizing her plants, trying to make sure that this time they did not die on her. She could never forget her embarrassment when she had taken one of her dried plants back to the nursery. The nursery assistant had taken one look at it and said,

'How did you manage *that*? It's pretty hard to kill these, it's one of the hardy natives,' and had burst out laughing at her mortified expression.

On Monday, during lunch Rene walked towards Crossword, her favourite bookstore on Pitt Street in the City. She usually enjoyed spending a few minutes lounging on one of the comfortable settees there, browsing through any book that sparked her interest. The purple of the Jacaranda flowers had carpeted the pavement and Sydney was awash with the colours of summer. Here and there the red flowers of the Illawarra flame tree made her stop with pleasure at the sight. As soon as she had walked a few steps and had passed the huge shop window, she stopped short. She walked back and sure enough, the flash of orange that she had caught out of the corner of her eye turned out to be *that* book.

Feeling that this must be some kind of sign, Rene entered the store and walked straight to where she had seen the book; and there it was, *The Hijras*, by Meher Pestonjee. She reached for the book a little hesitantly, as if it might jump up and bite her hand and as she touched it, she had the weirdest sense of opening a door, one from which there was no turning back.

Rene found a comfortable chair and opened the book. She flipped the first couple of pages to where the foreword was and looked for an explanation of the term *hijra*. On a side track of her mind, she wondered why she hadn't googled it.

There it was. She read:

The term 'hijra' is an Urdu word meaning eunuch or hermaphrodite. They are said to constitute a third gender category, considered by themselves and by others to be neither men nor women, and the archetypal hijra is raised as a man and undergoes ritual removal of the genitals to become a hijra. In reality, many hijras come from other sexually ambiguous backgrounds: they may be born intersexed, be born male or female and fail to develop fully at puberty, or be males who choose to live as hijras without ever undergoing the castration procedure. The cultural category 'hijra' appears to be a magnet for a variety of sexual and gender conditions: ambiguous sexual anatomy, impotence, infertility, homosexuality, and others which may not have an analogue in Western cultures.

Hijras are very diverse and most join the community as young boys. Discussed variously in the anthropological literature as 'transvestites', 'eunuchs', 'hermaphrodites', and even 'a third gender', most of India's hijras were raised as boys before taking up residence in one of the many hijra communities which exist in almost every region of India. A great number of hijras are men who identify themselves as more feminine than masculine and are forced by reasons such as familial rejection, cultural isolation and societal neglect to leave their families and find acceptance in these communities.

As she read, a channel in her brain heard a woman's voice saying something in a language she did not understand, except one word, hijra. A raw, razor sharp angry voice, a disturbing voice.

Rene kept rereading the lines, puzzled and confused. This was so completely weird. She had not known people like hijras existed. Of course, she had heard and read about cross dressers, transgenders and drag queens. Simone at her previous law firm had opted for sex change surgery and they had celebrated the event with drinks and cake when she returned as Simon. Rene had friends and workmates of both sexes who were gay. Still, they were in the periphery of her life and she certainly had never known or even met anyone who remotely resembled a hijra or even heard the term. *What, if any connection had this to do with her reality*, she wondered.

A shadow fell across the book and she looked up to see a shop assistant standing near her chair. The assistant was looking at her with a mixture of curiosity and concern.

'Can I help you?' she asked Rene.

'No, thank you, I'm good,' she replied.

She looked at her watch and saw that her lunch time was nearly up.

'Actually, I'd like to buy this book.' Rene said and walked with the assistant to the counter.

'You looked a little worried there. Seemed like you'd seen a ghost,' said the assistant chattily as she processed her receipt.

Rene stared at the assistant, as if the expression the girl had used should mean something to her. She paid for the book with her card and hurried to her office.

Rene caught the 6:39 evening train home and hurried impatiently to get to a seat quickly so that she could start reading the book. As she turned page after page, she became more and more fascinated by the lives of the hijras. Rene was shocked as she read about what most of the young boys quoted in the book had faced as they grew up in their parental homes and the circumstances that had forced them to run away from their families. Sadness smote her as she read about where they had to go, what they had to do in order to become accepted amongst their own kind.

Horrified by the dangerous procedures that some of them went through to make that transition irrevocable, Rene paused in her reading. She looked up to see the man sitting across from her staring at her curiously. A tear and slipped down her cheek and she wiped her eyes quicky, picking up her book. So engrossed in her book was she that she missed her stop and had to get off at the next one. While she waited for the train to go the other way in ten minutes, she bought a sandwich at the station cafe on the platform. She sat on a bench and as she did so, a strange thing happened.

Two images hovered in front of her, almost as if there was giant movie screen projected into the air. One was that of a young boy being shaken, almost dragged by the hand by a stern faced, grey haired woman, and she was screaming at the boy. The other was that of a little girl sitting with her mother in a small blue car, the same image she had seen in her dream a few days ago.

Rene stared stupidly at her half-eaten sandwich, as if wondering what it was doing in her hand.

This was no dream, she thought. *Why did I think of, no, not think, see those images? They seemed so real. Am I hallucinating?* She wondered.

Another idea chased that thought. *Did I have a past life? Is that what these images are?* She laughed, self-deprecatingly. She didn't really think so. The images were like photographs. *Oh my God, photographs!*

The train rumbled into the station and Rene got into it for the two-minute ride back to her stop in St Leonards. In her apartment, she heated water in the kettle and emptying the contents of a packet of soup into a cup, 'made' soup. Taking it along to the spare bedroom, she sipped as she went. There, she reached into one of the drawers where she had kept some old photographs.

Making herself comfortable on her favourite pod swing, Rene went through all the pictures she had seen so many times before. Some of these were black and white photographs of her parents; some were those of her as a little girl. There was nothing out of the ordinary there. Though why she was expecting to find something out of the ordinary, she couldn't really say.

****

CHAPTER 3

The Suitcase Spills a Secret

Rene sat back on the small round rug on the floor and peeked under the bed. *Ah, there it is!* That was where she had kept an old suitcase belonging to her father. It was one of the things she had brought from the house when he had passed away eight months ago. His lawyers had handed it to her saying that it had been in their custody and was to be given to her on his death. After his lawyers had settled his estate, she had moved into this apartment after leasing the house, finding it too big to live in on her own there.

In between dealing with her father's passing and starting a new job, Rene had forgotten all about the suitcase. A quick glance into the suitcase at the time had shown her some crayons, pencils, and an unfinished scarf. She had assumed they were some of her own things from her childhood.

Something made her hesitate before opening it, and something else was driving her to do just that. Her sudden movement while opening the lid made her clumsy, and the suitcase tipped over with half the contents on the floor beside her.

The first thing that caught her eye was an envelope whose edges were falling apart, showing a bundle of photographs through one torn edge. Rene undid the rubber band tied around the photos and looked through them. Some were black and white and some coloured. She stared at them, a puzzled frown wrinkling her smooth brow. She was quite sure she had never seen these photos before. There was one of a woman, middle-aged, very beautiful even at that age. A second picture was that of her grandmother, a woman with a serious, gaunt face and another of her grandfather, her dad's parents. There was another of the beautiful woman, this time with a man, probably her husband. Something about the woman's face was familiar.

Then, as she looked at the next one, shock rippled through her. It was her mother holding a baby in her arms and next to her, standing to her left, was a little boy, about six or seven years old. She stared at the boy as though at a ghost. She could have sworn he was the same boy she had seen in her mind's eye at the station. *This was probably the explanation for my recalling his face*, Rene supposed. But she paused in her thoughts; she was certain she had not seen this picture before. And why were they kept in a suitcase in her father's lawyers' custody? And who *was* this boy standing next to her mum with her arm around his shoulders?

There were more photos of the boy with her mum. One, when he was a toddler, being held high in the air, laughing into the camera and her mother laughing up at him. A studio photo with dad and mum and one more of the little boy with a baby in his lap was next. An arm with bangles was stretching out as if to make sure he didn't drop the baby. With a start, Rene realised that the baby was herself. Who was the *boy*, though? A brother she hadn't been told about? *Perhaps he had died and her parents had kept it from her*, she thought.

Something told her this was not so, though. At least when she had grown up, they would have told her, she reasoned. She had lived through losing her mother when she was seventeen; surely, she could have faced the truth about a brother whom she did not even remember?

Rene picked up some more photos scattered on the rug. There was another of the boy in school uniform – in dark blue shorts and a white shirt, a blue jacket with some kind of monogram on the pocket of the jacket. Then she picked up the last picture. In the centre was the same light blue car she had seen in her dream and in the vision flashing in her mind today. In front of it, with his right side towards the camera, was her dad holding something round and dark, his arm stretched above his head. He was bending in front of the car which had flowers on the bonnet. Off to one side, her mother was looking on, a baby, herself, tucked to her side. The little boy was sitting in the driver's seat, a big grin on his face.

Rene realised that it was a coconut in her father's hand and that he was in the act of breaking it in front of the car. That, and the flowers on the car, told her that this must be the *puja* for a new car, the prayers for invoking God's blessings for the wellbeing of the car and an auspicious beginning for the safety of its passengers in the future. In the distance she could see the dome of a temple.

She went over the photos many times in the next few minutes, all the time gazing intently at the boy holding her. There was something so very gentle in his expression that pulled at her heartstrings. A protective hand rested on the baby's chest and a smile tugged at a corner of his mouth. Only in one picture, where he seemed to be about ten years old, something a little sad seemed to lurk in his eyes. Her mother had turned a little as if to bring him nearer, whereas he looked like he wanted to put as much distance as he could from the camera. By this time, Rene's heart was thudding with the pained excitement of discovering what had so obviously been kept a secret.

A pink envelope caught her eye. In it was a thin sheet with flowers drawn all around like a border, a child's drawing. The paper was almost falling apart, and the writing was fading in places. It was titled "I am not in my own body" by Nimesha. Looking closely, Rene saw that the 'a' in the name had been crossed out. It was by Nimesh. She read,

"I am not in my own body"

By Nimesha

Trapped inside, a stranger to all but me
She asks to be let out, it is a plea
No one else hears her voice
Probably by choice
I cannot bear her cries for release
Yet I know I cannot please
Both her and those I love, who love me
To whom I then will be an oddity
But what can I do to let her out?
I am not in my own body; I want to shout.

There, the writing ended. It was a poem. It was an immaculate handwriting, very feminine, as were the flower drawings all around. The Rs were very like those in Rene's mum's recipe book, very typical of the cursive writing of people who had been to school in India. The alphabets were joined, with no gaps, which was also typical. It certainly was not anything she could have written. In any case, someone called Nimesh had written it.

Who was this Nimesh? Why were his things in dad's suitcase? A plastic folder caught her attention. Rene picked it up, and opening it, found three certificates. One was for a second prize in a fancy dress competition. The second was for participation in a dance competition. The third was a first prize for poetry writing. All the certificates were made out to 'master' Nimesh Ray Chaudhary.

Rene was about to shut the folder when she saw the corner of another paper sticking out from between two more of the certificates in one of the transparent plastic sleeves. Each certificate was facing the opposite side, with this one pushed in between. Unless you knew it was there, you would not normally have found it. Rene pulled it out gently. It was a birth certificate. It said:

Holy Family Hospital, New Delhi. Born: August 23rd 1987, To Mrs. Deepa Ray Chaudhary, a male child. Time: 3:40 PM.

The names were written in ink. The writing was quite clear. Deepa was Rene's mother's name. Rene had no doubts now. She had had an older brother that she had not been told about. Her hand holding the certificate trembled. The date of birth made him about seven years older than herself. There was no name for the baby, but then Rene knew that in India, names for babies were not mandatory at hospitals. A priest suggested an alphabet and parents named the child in elaborate naming ceremonies according to their religion and family tradition.

Stapled to the certificate were the patient's details, followed by the sex, weight, length and health information of the baby. The blood group came next, same as hers, B positive. There was also a very old cheque book, and a passport sized booklet which was oddly named Pass Book of The State Bank of India in the name of Nimesh Ray Chaudhary.

By this time, Rene's mind was in a whirl with the shocking discovery and she felt exhausted by the revelations. Desperately tired, she decided to go through the rest of the contents of the suitcase the next day. Taking the photo of the boy with herself in his lap, Rene propped it up against the clock on her bedside. For the first time in years, she remembered the imaginary friend she thought she had as a child. The memories were hazy. The friend had been so real to her, and she vaguely recalled talking to her. When she had grown older, Rene had thought, *I must have imagined a friend.* Probably brought on by the fact that she had been an only child, with no other children in the neighborhood, for the longest time. She looked at the picture and thought how similar the imagined expressions of the 'friend' and this boy were.

As she thought this, a shiver went up and down Rene's body. She found she was shaking. Oh my God, she thought, what if this boy was that friend? Her brother! Maybe her friend *wasn't* imaginary at all? She had reasoned that because she had not known about a brother, her naturally hazy memory given her age at the time had contrived to make him seem imaginary.

Only one piece did not fit the puzzle. Her friend had been a girl, of this she felt certain. So perhaps she *had*, in fact, been imaginary. That was her last thought as Rene dropped off into a deep, dreamless sleep.

****

CHAPTER 4

Making a Decision

Somewhere, the phone was ringing. Rene imagined she got out of bed, picked up the phone and said,

'Good morning, Rene here. Who is it?'

As she turned over, she realised with dismay that she had been fast asleep, and jack-knifed into a sitting position, eyes still closed. She felt for her phone on her bedside table, opened her eyes and saw from the time on the phone that she had overslept by a good two hours! The alarm on her phone had set off a mini dream in which she had heard it ringing and even had a conversation with someone.

Sometimes this happened to her. A stressful workload or physical exhaustion would cause a mini dream, as she called it, in which she had got up from bed and brushed her teeth, only to waken and realise she was still fast asleep! This was the first time it had happened on a working day, though.

Fortunately, she had nothing very important happening at work, so she called in sick. You did not just say that you had overslept if you wanted to continue in a prestigious law firm. Grimacing, Rene clamped down on her conscience and made a cup of strong ginger and cardamom tea for herself. She was in the mood to make it like her dad used to, with tea leaves, ginger, and cardamom chucked together into boiling water in a little saucepan. However, unlike him, she added the milk just at the end, before switching off the heat.

Rene took her tea out to her twelfth-floor balcony with its panoramic view of the cityscape and the Harbour Bridge. Rene never tired of looking at the water with the 'coat hanger' as the bridge was nicknamed. A Kookaburra laughed on a tree nearby as she tried to make sense of the secrecy surrounding her brother's existence. *Why hadn't her mother or her father ever told her about him?* She was guessing his name had been Nimesh. Perhaps her mother had found it too hurtful to talk about him, Rene thought. Maybe she had felt Rene was too young at first and then decided she would be better off not knowing. A memory Rene thought she had buried nagged her. She remembered her mother had cried achingly when she had thought no one heard, when she thought Rene was asleep, after tucking her in and sitting by her bed. But Rene had heard. And had also seen the faraway, despairing look in her eyes and wondered. When she had asked, her mother always said,

'I'm not feeling too well, sweetheart,' or 'I am just so tired, darling.'

When she died, Rene had thought that her mother had been ailing all along, and that finally her heart had failed.

But her dad had been a very practical, methodical man. Everything had to be in its proper place and well planned. If they went on a holiday, her dad would tick off all the items to be packed from a list he had made days before the trip. *Why hadn't he said anything?* Some years before he died, he had brought out all his papers related to bank deposits, investments, superannuation and the certificates of title of the house and apartments to let her know their financial condition 'just in case' anything happened to him. He was not the type of person who would not have told her about a brother who she did not even remember.

But he had not! So why *was* there such a mystery, *why?* Rene's head ached, her compulsion to know the truth punching holes in her head. She knew she had to look through everything in the suitcase to see if there was any clue, knew she would *not* rest until she found out more, knew that she had to uncover the truth behind this perplexing mystery.

Rene inserted a slice of raisin bread into the yellow toaster, made sure it was on the lowest setting, and waited for it to pop up. Rene wondered randomly why it was that raisin toasts always burnt more easily than other bread. She 'buttered' it with olive spread and remembered how she and dad had always argued over who had altered the setting and then forgotten to reset it. Dad had always liked his toast much darker, Rene mused.

After gulping down a glass of soy milk, Rene went in and got the suitcase out to the balcony. Placing it on the outdoor jarrah table, she sat cross-legged on one of the green and white striped, waterproof cushioned chairs and opened the suitcase. She took out the photos and examined each one, hoping to find some clue to the mystery. This time, the photograph of the beautiful middle-aged woman caught her attention. Both the man and the woman looked familiar. Of course! The man looked like her mother. The lines under his eyes told her that he was much older than mum, so he was probably her father, Rene's Nana. And the woman looked like an older version of her own self! They were surely her maternal grandparents! A rush of sadness and a rare feeling of nostalgia gripped Rene that they had never kept in touch after her mother had died. The last time she had seen them was before Rene moved to Australia. That is why she had not recognised them from their picture. *I am quite sure that I didn't see them on my last visit to India.*

There was a blue cloth bag with mirror worked embroidery in the suitcase, the kind made in Rajasthan or Gujarat in India. Inside was a note book, the edges timeworn. It was a math homework book. The name on the label said Nimesh Ray Chaudhary. The strangest thing was that, here too, the letter 'a' had been crossed out after the first name. All the answers seemed correct, there did not seem to be any mistake. Comments from the teacher such as 'well done', 'excellent work Nimesh' peppered all the pages. Her brother must have been a whiz at math, unlike herself!

A bittersweet smile curved her lips as she gazed at the collection of pencils, crayons, a scented eraser, a cracked flute, a pair of knitting needles, a half-knitted scarf still on one needle and a doll. Rene gazed absentmindedly at a small drawstring bag full of marbles, several art work sheets, mainly of flowers and children skipping and caressed a lock of fine baby hair in a zip lock bag. There was also a much thumbed story book – *Heidi* by Johanna Spyri.

Sitting there, staring at the Harbour bridge, Rene made up her mind. It was high time. She would visit her grandparents in India. Her gut feeling said that there was something not quite normal about her dad not being in touch with her mum's parents all these years, and vice versa. Added to which there was this mysterious brother about whom she was meant to discover in a suitcase full of mementoes!

Yes, there is something *very* odd here. *Why did dad leave all this for me to find after his death when he had been protecting me while he was alive?* He could easily have destroyed every last evidence of the existence of this brother! And the contents were exactly that – mementoes. But how was she supposed to find her grandparents? If they were still alive, that is.

Suddenly, an overwhelming sense of loneliness came over her, which she had not allowed herself to feel after her father had died. She had thought that if she kept the memories locked away, she would be able to cope. *And she had*, she believed, reasonably well. But it was as if something beyond reason was calling her to go back to her roots, to make sense of this puzzle.

Rene had always had what she referred to as her third eye. Once, while she was out of town for a conference in Melbourne, she imagined she saw her father falling. When she called him after returning to her hotel room, he laughed and making light of it, said,

'You are *such* a worrywart, grandma! It was just a small spill over a tree root. It was dark in that part of the trail. Don't you nag, I'll mend. Anyway, who told you?' It did not happen to her often, but one or two incidents that had happened in her dreams and thoughts had, in fact, taken place in reality. It scared her so much that she was afraid of her dreams. That was why Rene took her sixth sense seriously.

She went to check her passport to see if it was still valid. *Thank goodness, it is!* She had plenty of annual leave and she did not then care whether her firm could spare her. Rene wasn't normally impulsive, but worked very much with an animal like instinct. So far, it had worked well for her.

****

CHAPTER 5

Across the World

Rene rang Seema and then Helen to tell them she had booked her tickets to India and that she was flying next week. There was half a minute's silence from Seema before she said,

'I'm coming over.'

Helen said, 'Tarini, are you friggin' crazy? I'm coming over.' Helen only ever called her by her full given name when she was angry or upset with Rene.

They had been friends for too long not to know that something unusual was afoot in Rene's life. She had been to India only once after moving to Australia and had sworn never to visit again given her experiences on that one occasion. Rene had been sixteen and everything had seemed dirty and smelly. Men, old and young had tried to feel her up on public transport. She had hated the noise and the crowds. Her grandmother on her father's side had been alive then and made it a point to make her eat everything that she disliked. It had seemed that she made everything out of eggplant, brinjal as she called it, which she had known Rene could not stand.

'You must learn to eat everything, it's good for you. What will your in-laws say if you make such a fuss about everything?' she lectured Rene. Her grandmother had banned her from wearing shorts and skirts and Rene had suffered silently through the hot summer. Her dictum 'what will neighbours say?' moulded her every act.

Rene's cheeks had been pinched as if she had been five years old instead of sixteen and people whom she had never met had pestered her with questions like 'Did people have sex before they were married in Australia?' 'Did she have a boyfriend?' 'Had *she* had sex?' 'Did she consider herself an Aussie or an Indian?' 'Did the Aussies treat her like one of them? Or was she treated badly by the *goras*?'

'Were they not racist?' 'Were they not a terribly free society, with people running around nude on the beaches and drinking beer all day, watching cricket?'

At the end of the two month 'holiday', Rene felt that she was an alien in her own country of origin and couldn't wait to get back to Sydney. On her return, she felt only relief and safe in her familiar surroundings, which she had so far taken for granted. There was no way she could have made those people questioning her understand that she was equally comfortable with her friends of Indian background as well as her *gora* friends. Nor could she explain footy to cricket lovers.

It was no wonder then that both Helen and Seema felt that something was seriously the matter with Rene. Helen said as much to Seema when she met her at the entrance to the lifts.

'I knew something was up. Rene has always seemed very preoccupied of late while talking to me, and when I try to get to the bottom of it, she's quick to end the conversation,' she confided to Seema.

Seema had brought a particular brand of Cabernet Sauvignon that Rene liked and Helen held a bunch of fragrant white Liliums in her arms, Rene's favourite flowers. Their greeting was a little subdued, both Helen and Seema fixing Rene with penetrating stares. Rene buried her face in the Liliums, savouring their fragrance. Each of the girls homed in on her favourite seat, Helen on the Zebra print bean bag, Seema on the white chaise and Rene in the egg-shaped pod swing.

'Let's fix priorities,' said Helen and picked up the phone.

'Thai Phoon Restaurant? It's me Helen. Yep, from Rene's place. Yes, the usual. One pad thai, no peanuts on top, chilli basil stir fry with chicken – extra hot. Rice. No, wait.' she raised her brows to the dumb charade by Rene. 'Oh. No rice. We have that. Jasmine rice has a very high GI. What? You don't use ghee? No, no, GI, glycemic index. No worries, it's ok, no rice. Green curry prawn and snake beans in olive sauce. In fifteen minutes? Excellent! Thanks.'

Helen, by now, had the giggles very badly, and the three were rolling with laughter.

'Dudes! Could you not giggle around me when I'm talking on the phone? Ghee! How was I to explain GI?' Helen said and broke off into another fit of laughter.

Wiping tears of laughter, Rene got up to get some wine glasses, beer nuts, chilli flavoured potato chips and a plate of carrot and celery cut into thin slices. Seema had brought her favourite beetroot dip and they once again settled down, chatting with the ease of friends who didn't have to pretend with each other.

They were interrupted by the young man buzzing the door to deliver their food and for a while the three foodies concentrated on piling their plates and making sure they had the tastes exactly right. Seema added extra chili sauce, while Rene added a good splash of fish sauce. Helen, as usual, mixed soy sauce and fresh chillies in a bowl for everyone and added an enormous amount to her share.

'Your ability to eat spicy food never ceases to amaze me,' Rene said to Helen, her own eyes watering.

The girls went back to their respective spots with their plates and after two or three chopsticks full of food, Helen said,

'All right, let's have it, Rene. What's with this damn fool idea of haring off to India so suddenly?'

Seema added, 'Didn't you always say that you'd never go back? What's with this sudden plan? And that too in a *week's* time?' This last came out in a squeak.

Rene knew that she would have to tell her friends everything, only none of it hardly made sense to *her*. She opened her mouth to speak, but stopped. Instead, she went to the photo on her bedside table and brought the suitcase with her. She handed these to Helen. Seema moved over and the two looked through them, puzzled frowns wrinkling their brows.

By this time, they had finished eating and Rene had cleared the coffee table, while Seema had cleared out the garbage. Helen elected to help with the dishes. She looked up from the photos and said,

'I am guessing this has to do with your trip and there is this mystery boy here who is the reason. But who is he?'

'My brother. My brother Nimesh,' said Rene baldly.

At this, Seema made a grab for the photos again and said,' You don't, you didn't have a brother. What are you talking about?' Helen only stared as if Rene had somehow lost her mind.

'I am in shock myself, Seema. Look at the birth certificate. The pics. They were all in a suitcase kept in Dad's lawyers' office. What I can't fathom is why Dad didn't tell me himself, leaving me to find out like this. He, my brother that is, is probably not even alive,' Rene tried to explain.

'Obviously! Why would he not be here with you if he were alive? In that case, why bother going? What do you expect to find out there? Best leave it alone, Rene,' Helen advised.

Seema laughed, 'Unless they put him in an asylum.' And then she suddenly sobered up, just in case that was true.

Helen flapped her fingers at her and scolded, 'Don't be a clown, Seema. Not now. Can't you see she's stressed already?' Then she turned to Rene, saying, 'This is so weird. I can imagine that you are in shock, mate. Even so, let sleeping dogs lie, I say!'

Even as she said so, a thought troubled her. *If she herself had been in a similar situation, she would have wanted to do the same as Rene, wouldn't she?*

Seema added, 'I don't understand why your dad didn't tell you either, Rene. Maybe he found it hard to accept, however tough he appeared on the outside, and couldn't tell you. I don't know. Just accept it and let it go, Rene. Maybe the circumstances of your brother's death were such that...' She stopped. She realized she was making things worse, not better.

'For argument's sake, accepting that you need to find out for yourself, how on earth would you go about it? Who is there to help you? How would you find out anything about him? You said your gran is not alive, and that you had no family back in India except your one distant *cousin*. With whom you haven't been in touch since you were ten. And where would you stay? Not alone, in some hotel... surely?' Helen chimed in, her worry clearly showing in her eyes.

Rene said, 'I will have to begin where I was last, I suppose. And that's New Delhi. I really haven't thought it through. I am not even sure whether my mum's parents are still alive or where they live, even. Dad never kept in touch with them, you know. But I know from what dad said that my cousin Jai is the CEO of a group of companies, very well known, actually. It shouldn't be too difficult to trace him. He is not really related to me, strictly speaking. His mum's brother's wife is my dad's sister. So, my dad's sister is his aunt only by marriage, so to speak.'

She could see Helen rolling her eyes at the description. Helen could never understand the Indian penchant for calling the parent of every friend and even some complete strangers aunty or uncle. Rene and Seema had tried to explain to her that it was something like the indigenous Australians' closeness to their extended families. And that it was a mark of respect to call everyone in their parents' generation likewise. That to call them by their first names or with a formal mister or Mrs. would be rude. But she *still* did not get it.

Both Seema and Helen could see that Rene was completely set on going on this mission as they thought of her plan privately, and that there was no dissuading her.

Seema thought for a minute and making up her mind, said, 'If you have to go, there's no need to stay in a hotel. My grandmother would gladly have you; you know that. Quite apart from the fact that you went out of your way taking her on a Sydney tour and a zillion fun outings when I was out of action with my fractured leg last year, she thinks the world of you. She thinks I should be more like you, though I can't see why.' Seema ducked a cushion as she said this and added, 'Dadi would mind terribly if you stayed in a hotel when she has this indecently huge bungalow and some three, four people waiting on her hand and foot. May I use your phone?'

She dug into her wallet and fished out a phone card, which allowed her some two hundred and fifty minutes for calls to India. While she was punching the long string of numbers, Helen found the coffee mugs and put the kettle on. Rene took out some frozen apple danish and stuck it in the oven. She could hear Seema talking to her Dadi, asking and answering a million questions before talking about Rene's forthcoming visit. Seema turned to her and beckoned, handing her the phone.

'What is this *beta*, what do I hear about you wanting to stay in a hotel? Am I *dead*? Don't I have this vast house crying for people to live in it? Let me have none of this nonsense. You will stay with me. And, just in case you feel obliged, you can make me that wonderful sticky date pudding while you are here. With that, how do you say it? Awesome, yes awesome sauce!' So saying, Dadi let out a peal of laughter.

Despite herself, Rene smiled. Anyway, her accommodation was settled, for as long as she wanted. Over hot apple danish topped with vanilla ice cream and a mug of steaming coffee, the three girls went to work on the laptop, checking out the weather in Delhi and deciding what Rene should take with her on her trip. Suddenly, Rene did not feel so alone in her quest and the uncertain journey looming ahead of her seemed a little less confronting.

****

CHAPTER 6

New Delhi

The trip itself was uneventful, which was welcome. Since it was off peak and not holiday season, there were quite a few seats empty. Rene found four unoccupied ones in a row in the middle section of the plane. Pushing back the arm rests, she stretched out and settled the beige blanket around herself. She remembered her boss's reaction to her trip with a certain amount of glee. He had been so shocked at her announcement that she was going off on a long holiday that he had stared at the paralegal standing near as though for an explanation. Then, deciding from her manner that she would go anyway, he had decided to be nice about it. Rene knew he was also dying of curiosity, so she had said,

'There is something I need to do, something I have to do. It's all very complicated but when I have settled what I am going to India for, I'll come back. It has something to do with my father's matters. But it's all very iffy, so I don't expect you to hold the position for me. I would appreciate a reference though.'

As soon as she was off the plane and had collected her baggage, she headed for the exit through customs. She had to fight off a few very determined 'helpers' who were very sure that she wouldn't be able to pick up her suitcase from the baggage conveyer.

Rene looked around with pleasant surprise at the New Delhi airport, very much like the Singapore airport she had been waiting in during her two-hour stopover in the twelve-hour flight. She was sure that it had not been this nice on her last trip, and it certainly did not smell of the strong disinfectant she so clearly remembered almost fainting from – the last time she was here.

Two of the airport shops caught her attention. Rene browsed through the interesting figurines and lovely handicrafts and made a mental note to herself to buy something for her friends from there on her return to Sydney.

Rene groaned seeing the long queue at immigrations and when she reached his desk the dour faced immigration clerk stared at the passport and her and asked her a lot of irrelevant questions before finally letting her through. Under her breath, she muttered,

'A smile won't cost you, mate.' As she stood uncertainly near the exit, in a hall full of taxi rental, travel agent and money exchange cubicles, a grey-haired lady travelling alone asked,

'You seem to be new here. Is someone coming to pick you up?'

'Yes,' said Rene, 'only I don't know which way to go. It all looks very confusing.'

'Come this way dear,' the lady said, and Rene followed her to the exit. The heat hit her instantly despite the time of the year, and as she rolled her trolley down a concrete ramp, she saw a few people carrying name cards. Straight away, she saw her own name on one of them, and, after thanking the lady, she walked towards the man holding the card.

His name was Shyam Singh, and he was Manju *memsaab's* driver, he said. Manju was Seema's grandmother's name. He insisted on taking the baggage trolley from her, shocked that she should think of pushing it herself. By the time Rene reached the car, her top was sticking to her back. Shyam Singh saw her wiping her face and neck and, smiling broadly with shining white teeth in a dark brown face, said,

'No problem, madam, car having AC. You cool in no time.'

'Thank you, Shyam,' Rene said, and he looked taken aback, not used to being addressed by his first name by employers or their guests. It was either driver *ji* or *bhaiya* or Shyam Singh.

Rene tried to take in as much of the scenery as she could in the dark, but most of it was a blur of lights in the heavy smog. She saw many trucks, and Shyam Singh informed her it was because they travelled mostly at night.

'It is tradition *Memsaab,* for the drivers to decorate their trucks with dazzling, even gaudily coloured lights. Brings good luck,' explained Shyam Singh when Rene remarked on the overdressed, brightly lit trucks.

Manju Dadi's house was in a suburb called Maharani Bagh in South Delhi, quite far from the airport. Rene had the impression of an interesting fort like structure on the way and what looked like a mosque before they entered a relatively wider street, stopping in front of tall, scrolled iron gates set in the middle of high white walls. There was some kind of pretty creeper growing all over the walls, cascading down like a green waterfall. Two bright lamps topped the columns on either side of the gate.

As soon as the car stopped, a man came out of a little guard room on the inside of the gates, next to a curving driveway. He opened the heavy gates, which rolled effortlessly on well-oiled wheels. Shyam Singh drove through and stopped under a wide portico. The house was an imposing structure, built in a very *haveli* like architectural style and completely white, except for the green, tiled roof. There were red and pink flowers blooming in bunches on a climbing Rangoon creeper with yellowish green leaves on one side of the portico, while the twisting branches of a lilac wisteria shrub graced the other. The whole effect took Rene's breath away; it was so beautiful. Numerous potted plants lined the veranda, and the smell of jasmine was strong. Rene decided she would have to explore the garden in the daylight.

Meanwhile, the door was opened to Shyam Singh's pull on the rope of an antiquated brass bell. A woman in a green sari stood there, her hands joined in a traditional *namaste*. She bobbed her head once in salutation. Rene responded likewise. The woman led Rene through the arched opening to the left of the entrance hall into the sitting room. There, sitting on the seat of a huge, beautifully carved wooden Gujarati swing, was Manju Dadi, her face wreathed in a huge smile, her arms outstretched in loving welcome.

Rene walked to her and was embraced like a long-lost child. She had to swallow a few times to hold back tears. She hadn't expected such a warm welcome. Holding Rene's hands in her own wrinkled ones Dadi said,

'I am so happy to see you, my dear. I was so looking forward to your visit. I would have come to the door to welcome you to my home, but this evening my knee is giving me a lot of trouble. A touch of the old osteoarthritis, beta. I hope you will be comfortable here, child. And you must feel free to come and go as you wish. Seema has informed me about the purpose of your visit and I sincerely hope that you find out what happened to your brother. Only, I am afraid that you may find that it is a difficult, if not an impossible task.'

She patted the seat of the swing next to her, inviting Rene to sit amongst the brightly coloured and delicately embroidered cushions. After chatting with her for some time, Dadi shooed Rene away to have a shower as if she was a little girl. Rene had already phoned ahead to say that she would have her dinner on the flight and after changing into her pajamas, fell asleep almost instantly, the time difference making sure of that.

****

CHAPTER 7

'Cousin' Jai

Rene awoke to the sound of a cock crowing. Of all things, she thought, amused and a little dazed. Feeling completely disoriented, she looked around the strange room, vaguely at first, taking a few seconds to remember where she was. The windows were open and an early morning breeze was blowing in the white embroidered muslin curtains. A strange whirring sound above her made her look up, and she saw the most beautiful ceiling fan she had ever seen. It had been crafted out of white rattan and she worried it was going too fast. In Sydney, the few ceiling fans she had seen seemed to move at a snail's pace. A white mosquito net draped the sides of the four-poster bed and someone had let it down and tucked in the sides after she had gone to sleep. A feeling of peace stole over her, and she lay in bed for another hour, thinking, what the heck, she didn't have a train to catch.

Then, feeling it would be rude to be late for breakfast, Rene threw off the blue and white Jaipuri bedspread. She looked at her bedside clock and was surprised to find that it was only five in the morning! Of course, she thought, it would be about nine – thirty in Sydney.

The bathroom was enormous, with a sunken tub on one side and the taps and shower head opposite. There was a curious looking white drum like container high on the wall above the tub, which Dadi had explained was a geyser. That supplied the hot water in the bathroom. Near the door there was a big, black, carved dresser with a swing mirror. Someone had thought to pile it with lotions, soaps and a variety of perfumes. Across from that was the sink, a commode and a bidet. Rene felt there was still enough room to for her to dance in. She felt sure that her room must be the master bedroom with this gigantic 'ensuite'!

Breakfast was in the balcony just off Dadi's bedroom. On one side, a climbing Indian jasmine lent its lovely scent to the morning.

Dadi's balcony looked down into a small walled courtyard with a square, intricately scrolled stone pot in the centre. Looking closely, Rene saw that the huge 'pot' was actually fixed to the ground and had a sacred basil *tulsi* plant growing in it. A narrow, paved path snaked away from the pot. At the end of the walkway stood a fountain – a sandstone Khajuraho dancing girl smiling sensuously, water gurgling from an urn in her arms.

As she looked, Dadi walked to the tulsi plant in her usual freshly laundered, starched white sari of hand loomed cotton and folded her hands in prayer. This was her daily ritual after her shower in the morning. She looked up at Rene, smiled, and waved. In a few minutes, she joined her at breakfast – a delectable spread of hot stuffed potato *parathas*, pickle and curd. Rene thought that if she had these every day, she would shortly resemble the stuffing in the bread. She said as much to Dadi.

Dadi laughed and said, 'Don't worry, you are so thin, it will not matter. But from tomorrow, just tell Ramdhani our cook what you want – toast, eggs, cereal, he will have it ready for you.'

Over coffee, they discussed the best way to try to locate Jai, her 'cousin'. Rene did not know which company or companies he was CEO of, nor did she know his last name, so she hadn't bothered trying to find him on the net.

Shortly after breakfast Rene went exploring in the walled garden she had seen from her window, while Dadi went to instruct the cook about lunch and the gardener about some annuals she wanted planted in pots for her courtyard. After that she planned to call some friends who, according to her, were sure to find out Jai's whereabouts.

The walled garden with its green waterfall creeper had been Dadi's husband's handiwork while he had been alive. It was cleverly simple. Just one very tall Gul Mohur tree with scarlet flowers stood somewhere in the middle, near one side of the wall. Some carved stone benches were placed around the edges of a beautiful and well maintained lawn with a riot of flowers all around it. Some pots hung from the branches of the tree, with green succulents and lilac coloured flowers trailing downwards.

****

While they were having their afternoon tea of hot samosas, a call came for Dadi from one of her husband's friends. She came back excited and smiling. She said to Rene,

'It was Ajay bhaisaab, and he rang to say that he had Jai's company address and phone number.'

Dadi urged Rene not to waste any time and asked her to phone Jai straight away as soon as she knew who he was.

'Why didn't you tell me it was that Jai, Jayant Miglani? He is not a CEO of one company, my dear, but a family of them. We knew his father; he had been an IPS officer and pretty high in the Delhi police hierarchy until a few years ago. He will be of great help in finding out where your grandparents might be, if they're still alive, that is,' added Dadi softly.

Rene swallowed the rest of her tea and headed for the phone. The number she rang was the switchboard one; a polite, impersonal voice connected her to a secretary called Mrs. Batliwala. A friendly voice said,

'Jai Miglani's office. How can I help you?' Rene introduced herself briefly and said,

'I am his cousin, from Australia. Could I speak to him, please?' It took five calls at half-hour intervals to get through to him. Mrs. Batliwala answered the last call with an,

'I am sorry, but Jai has many cousins, if you know what I mean. Could I have a name, please?'

'Sure, it's Rene or Tarini, but I doubt he'll remember the name. I really am a sort of cousin, not one of his myriad girlfriends, trying to trick you into putting me through.'

Rene could hear the secretary relay the message verbatim to Jai and she presumed it intrigued him enough to take the call.

'Hi cousin Rene, Jai here.' The accent was on the word cousin.

'Hi. You probably don't remember me. I used to live here years ago. My Yamini *bua*, dad's sister, is your *mami*.'

'Hmm, Yamini mami, your bua, let's see, I don't… of course! I get it! You were that little pigtailed brat who used to run away with my new bike! Why didn't you say you were Dimpy? That is your nickname, isn't it? I *do* remember you. But how come you decided to get in touch after all this time? You guys just disappeared into the ether, so to speak,' Jai answered.

Rene's eyes clouded over at the childhood nickname. No one but her parents had called her that and she had almost forgotten that anyone had called her that, ever.

'Yes, well, it's a long story,' she replied. 'The simple truth is, I need to find out some missing bits about my family, and you were the only person I could remember who might have a clue as to the whereabouts of my grandparents. It appears, though, that you are an extremely busy man and I don't really want to impose. Frankly, I had no one else to ask.'

There was what seemed to Rene, a significant pause and then, Jai's crisp but lovely voice said,

'Okay, I'll be finished here in a couple of hours. If I come and pick you up from Maharani Bagh, it'll take close to an hour and a half at that time. If you can meet me at, say, South Extension, we can grab a bite and I can drop you back after. Does that sound doable?'

Rene asked Dadi if she could borrow Shyam Singh and the car for the evening and hurried to her room to shower and change. She wore jeans and one of the many kaftan style cotton tops she had bought from an Indian clothes store in Sydney. She found them pretty and comfortable, given the high humidity in the air.

****

CHAPTER 8

Kasauli

Rene was amused to find Jai twirling his car keys as he had said he would, to make it easy for her to recognise him. She hadn't taken him seriously, and there he was doing exactly that, leaning against his car, a tall, slim man with thick, straight hair, warm brown eyes in a very arresting face. He straightened when he saw her and his smile as he shook hands made her think, this one's a charmer, no wonder he had so many 'cousins' ringing him up, even at work!

Rene knew she was good looking; she had been told that too many times not to; but she had never thought about her looks much. The appreciative gleam in Jai's eyes as he greeted her made her glad somehow.

'Hi cousin Rene,' he said, smiling a little as he said so. 'Wow, you have grown up and beautiful too. I was expecting pigtails. Hope you're hungry cause I'm starving. I only had four sandwiches with my tea over an hour ago.' When he saw her eyes widen, he said, 'I have this very high metabolism, you see. My friends call me Jughead because I'm hungry all the time. Do you like Chinese food?' When she said yes, she did, he took her arm and said, 'There's a good Chinese restaurant here called Daitchi,' and guided her there.

After they had ordered their drinks and food, Jai sat back and said, 'So Dimpy, tell me about yourself as in, you know, fill in the blanks from when you left India.'

'There's not much to tell, really. The usual new immigrant journey. I joined school in Sydney in year three, then went to high school, followed by a double degree in commerce and law at Sydney Uni. I have been working as a solicitor in a small law firm in the city for the last four years,' said Rene.

'All work and no play?' quipped Jai.

'Hardly. Apart from school and Uni, I enrolled in the various activities kids my age usually do during their school days – learned ballet for some years, played netball, learnt Kathak dancing and the piano. And flute. Oh yes, gymnastics. I was quite a decent backstroke swimmer too,' Rene finished. She did not add that she had been a state gold medalist and smiled at the look on his face.

Jai laughed, 'Wow, that's a long list! Impressive! All that in one person! What happened? I mean, what about your parents? How did your mum…. I am sorry, I know your dad passed away last year, but I hadn't known about your mum.'

'She had a heart attack when I was seventeen years old,' replied Rene quietly.

'I am sorry. It was just that your grandparents never seemed to mention you all whenever we met them. It was strange, to say the least. All these years and they haven't mentioned any of you until early this year when your dad's solicitor informed them about his passing,' Jai said, his voice soft.

Rene jumped. 'Are they still alive, then? Are you in touch with them?'

Jai stared at her in surprise. She was terribly embarrassed. She rushed to tell him how, after her mother had died, they had simply lost touch. How she had shut her mind to everything related to her mother's death and that when she had later tried to talk to her father, she had found that he was very reluctant to talk about her grandparents. She had assumed that after losing their daughter, they had not kept in touch. She did not know whether they were alive, where they lived, or whether they would even want to see her.

'But why now?' asked Jai.

Rene sighed and told him about the contents of the case and her startling discovery of her brother, Nimesh.

'And now my only hope of finding out what happened to him, why there is this mystery surrounding his death, is by finding my grandparents. If I can find them, that is. If they want to see me,' she finished.

Jai looked at the sadness in her eyes and resolved to himself that he would try to do everything in his capacity to help her. Rene's honesty and resolve touched a chord in him and he recognised a kindred spirit, a fighter for what they wanted. He said,

'I am sure they are alive unless something, God forbid, has happened in the last six months. I'll tell you what I'll do. I will ring

Yamini mami and get their address for you. She's sure to have it.' He took out his cell phone as he spoke and found the number he was looking for. After a few seconds Rene could hear a high-pitched female voice before Jai switched off the speaker and said,

'*Pranam mami*. Yes, yes, I am fine. Yes, I know I have been bad. But I promise to call more often. No, seriously dear aunt! But I have something important to tell you now. You can scold me later. Guess who I am having dinner with, mami? Dimpy, no less. From Sydney. Yes. Oh, it's a long story, but not mine to tell. You can have it from her when you meet her. Do you have her Nana's address? Where are they now? Hmm. Interesting. Could you please text it to me? Thanks. My regards to that lazy uncle of mine. Too hard to pick up the phone and ring, huh? Remind him that mom is his only sister. Yes, yes, I will drop in. That's not a bad idea, but I'll ask Dimpy whether she is okay with it first. See you soon. Take care.' Jai turned to Rene.

'Well, the interesting part is that your Nana and Nani have moved to their family home in Kasauli only six months ago. That is also near where I went to school, in Sanawar. It isn't very far, maybe five or six hours' drive from Delhi. It is a beautiful hill station and they've retired there. Yamini mami didn't have their phone number though. She said she wrote it down on a magazine while speaking to them and has since lost it.' Jai rolled his eyes expressively. 'The house she remembered from her visits there when she was a new bride and from holidays, so she knew the name of the street, at least. I believe that all I have to do is stand in front of the house of the given description and shout out your Nani's name, and we're done,' he supplied.

Rene wasn't sure what she felt. A kind of trepidation mixed with hope. Trepidation about her reception by her grandparents when she eventually met them. About what she would feel when she saw them. Hope that here at last was a connection to her past with the possibility of finally finding out the truth about her brother Nimesh. She knew, of course, that she would travel to Kasauli to meet them. After refusing dessert, she walked back with Jai to the car.

'What now?' asked Jai. 'I assume you would want to meet them?'

'Of course! I'll need to book a car for Kasauli, right? I'll do that tomorrow. If I leave early Friday morning, I could even be back by elevenish, I think.'

'Mmm. Not a good idea travelling alone in a cab by yourself so late.' He made a spur of the moment decision. 'Look, if you can wait one more day, I can come with you on Saturday. After all, you are a sort of relative, if not strictly a cousin. I would feel truly responsible if something happened to you. I can look up one of my old teachers while I am there and a few of my girlfriends, too. 'Course, if you don't like the idea of my coming with you, at least take my car and driver. I think though, that it might help reduce some of the trepidation you are feeling in meeting them if I'm there with you.'

It was on the tip of Rene's tongue to refuse his offer, but she realised the truth of his perception. And, even in the little time she had spent with Jai, she had figured Jai wasn't one of those smooth kinds of men. There was a certain seriousness about him despite his bantering manner, a purposefulness that told her he didn't run his companies just by being a playboy.

'I would be glad if you would. But it seems like putting you in an awful lot of trouble. I...' she hesitated.

'No trouble. Ok. It's decided then. He opened the car door for her to get in. I'll be at your place at, let's see, seven thirty good for you?'

She agreed as they drove off. Jai saw her to Dadi's door and said a quick namaste to Dadi, who was waiting up for her out of curiosity. It certainly satisfied her to have met the legendary Jai finally. Jai read all this at a glance, said a grinning good night to both and took his leave, while Rene wondered what was so funny. She asked him as she went to see him off, to which he whispered,

'She was sussing me out with meaningful looks at you and me.' At her blank look, he said, rolling his eyes, 'I forgot you're an Aussie. As a prospective groom, read me, for a prospective bride, read you.' With eyes laughing at her look of dismay, he said, 'Goodnight Dimpy, I mean Rene.'

'Goodnight. You really are a rascal, as I first thought. You can call me Dimpy, I don't mind. See you Saturday.'

'Yup. See you.' And he was off, jogging down the driveway.

****

CHAPTER 9

The Secret is in the Poem

Jai looked surprised to find her ready and waiting for him with her case when he arrived on the dot at seven thirty on Saturday morning.

'Not used to the women in my life being punctual,' he explained.

'Oh, I'm flattered,' Rene said.

'What for? That I think you're punctual?'

'No, that I am a woman in your life,' she answered with a grin.

'Just so you know how lucky you are,' Jai grinned back. He lifted her case onto the boot of the car and they set off with Dadi waving them off.

Rene was surprised to find that for the most part, the road was wide and two laned. For the first two hours, there were very few of the big trucks and Jai pointed out some interesting places with funny anecdotes about his boyhood spent travelling on the same roads, term after term. He was very witty; his stories were interesting and time flew and the journey lost most of its tension for Rene.

They stopped for lunch at a road-side inn called a *dhaba* locally. It was traditionally a stopping place for truck drivers, but now an extremely popular eating place with travellers and residents of nearby towns. Rene took out the sandwiches and bottled water that Ramdhani had packed for her, looking doubtfully at the tandoori chapati and chicken curry Jai was devouring with great gusto, although her mouth watered at the aroma.

Later, the road became one laned and the way in which the driver was driving had Rene on the edge of her seat, sure that they would crash any minute. He would drive on the wrong side for whole stretches of the road, before suddenly swerving onto the left lane from right in front of an enormous truck at the last minute. Seeing her face, Jai touched the driver's shoulder.

'Bhola, could you please drive in your own lane? We want to reach Kasauli in one piece. We are in no tearing hurry to meet our maker,' he said.

'I noticed you are quite calm about it. Doesn't it bother *you*?' Rene said, glancing at him curiously.

'In India you learn to be stoic in all circumstances,' Jai replied with a smile. 'Actually, I am used to it. Almost everyone drives like this on the highways here.' He saw her peering at the back of the truck in front of her and on enquiring found that she was trying to read what was written on the back. He read and translated,

'O you of evil eye, your face is black.' Rene was fascinated with the brightly decorated trucks and was in splits as he read and translated the different messages, which seemed to be mandatory adornment on the back of every truck she saw. Some were inspirational and some simply hilarious. 'Life of the rich, biscuits and cake', 'life of a truckie, clutches and brake,' 'take poison but don't believe in girls,' 'overtake me if you have the balls or else tolerate being stuck behind my ass,' 'life is drama, man is actor' and many like that made the trip seem like a fun game and, before Rene knew it, they were on the outskirts of Kasauli.

Rene looked with pleasure at the beautiful and quaint little town with its cobbled paths, nineteenth century shops, its colonial ambience reinforced by gabled houses and charming facades. She looked upon neat little gardens and orchards and inhaled the fresh scent of the fragrant pine, refreshing after the pollution in Delhi. Giant Himalayan oak, huge horse chestnuts and rolling grassland were all together, a feast to the eyes. Its narrow roads curving up and down the hillsides punctuated with red and green roofed, white houses, made Kasauli a lovely sight to behold. It was one of the small towns developed by the British as a hill station during the days of their Raj, Jai explained to her.

The car turned into a narrow, cobbled street and stopped almost immediately in front of a picturesque, white wooden house with a red, tiled roof. The roof looked like it needed a lick of paint but was charming for all that, especially with white wisteria climbing up on one side of the house, right up to the roof. A glossy leafed creeper, with bunches of deep red flowers, graced the other side. Rene had never seen them before, and Jai informed her they were Flaming Glories.

'This must be it,' Jai said and pulled on a little rope bell to the side of the green shuttered door. There was no electric bell. When he heard footsteps coming, he pushed Rene to one side with a finger to his lips. There was the sound of a door opening on the inside, and then the outer doors were opened by a slim, tall woman in a blue salwar suit. She still carried with grace the remnants of a stunningly beautiful face, now faded with age. A smile lit up her face as she saw Jai.

'*Arre* Jai beta, what a lovely surprise! How come? Are you here on some business? Oh, look at me, asking all this at the door! Come in son, I am so pleased to see you. Let's see, it must be more than a year since I last saw you. Let me wake up uncle.' Her voice lowered as they went inside and Rene felt a bit silly waiting outside when all she wanted was to see her grandparents desperately. Just then, she heard Jai saying,

'Wait a minute Auntie, I have a surprise for you. You will never guess who it is!'

He was back at the door in less than a minute and was leading Rene in, saying as they reached the puzzled and curious Nani,

'Here she is.'

Nani stared at Rene for what seemed like a long time. She took Rene's hand in hers, her eyes filling with tears.

'It can't be. But of course, I must believe my eyes. Oh my God, at last.' She seemed lost in thought. 'At last, you have come to me, my child. I have been waiting so long for this day,' she sighed. Rene felt her own eyes pricking.

'Do you know who I am?' she asked.

'How could I not? I have had this strange feeling for days now that it will not be long before Dimpy comes looking for us, and you have. Oh my God, Dimpy.' Nani's voice broke with her pent up emotion. She drew Rene forward into her arms. Rene felt that she had come home. She could feel Nani's body shake as she hugged her and silent tears coursed down her own cheeks. Suddenly, Nani laughed and said,

'We should be celebrating, not crying, child! Let's go inside. Come, Jai.' Nani led them both to the living room just inside and to the right of the hallway. It was furnished with simple yet elegant white rattan lounges with cream and green cushions. On the floor was a handmade dhurrie of pastel pinks and greens on a cream background. Fresh pink hydrangeas graced crystal vases.

Nani could not seem to let go of Rene's hand and drew her to one of the rattan two seaters to sit with her. There was a charming window seat and Jai lounged on it, looking at both of them with a curious smile.

'And look at you, Tarini beta. You are just like I was at your age. Come here. See this picture.' It was a black and white photograph in a silver frame on a side table by their chair. The photographer had touched it up to look like a painting, as was common in the time it was taken.

'The only difference is that I had long hair, almost to my knees,' Nani continued. 'And the clothes are different too, of course! But both my daughter's children look like me.' She stopped, shocked at what she thought she had let slip.

Rene touched Nani's arm and said, 'Don't worry Nani, my brother's existence is not a secret anymore. I know I had a brother.' She related how she had discovered the photographs in the suitcase. 'This is the reason I have come after all these years, Nani. To find out what happened to him. You see, all this time I did not know how to contact you, whether you were still....' she stopped.

'Alive.' finished Nani. 'This suitcase,' she asked. 'You say your father left it for you. Have you brought it with you?'

'Yes, I have the contents here. What I can't understand is the secrecy surrounding my brother's existence. What actually happened, Nani? Did he die? Why has no one ever told me?' Rene asked as she took out the contents of the case. Jai watched as the two women, the older a faded and still lovely version of the younger, went through the contents together. Nani was reading the poem written by Nimesh. She read it once more, aloud. As she reached the end, Nani burst into tears.

'The secret is in this poem, child, she said as she looked at her granddaughter. Read it carefully. See how the name has been changed to Nimesha?' She said when she had quietened.

Rene looked blankly at Nani. 'I don't understand,' she said.

'No, you don't. How can you?' answered Nani. She sighed and looked confused, as if she did not know how to explain. She looked across at Jai. There was dawning comprehension struggling with disbelief in his eyes, and Rene saw it too.

At that very moment, there was a knock on the door, and Nani got up with relief to let in a short, stout man of indeterminate age and a dark, cheerful countenance. His smile showed white teeth in a dark brown face, his eyes round with curiosity as he looked at Rene. He joined his hands in greeting to Jai, whom he knew, and then greeted Rene. By now Rene had learnt from Seema's Dadi that one did not automatically shake hands or hug someone as soon as they were introduced, so she kept to her chair. Nani introduced him as Ramu, the cook cum general dogsbody, who had lived with her family since he was a little boy. When Nani told him who Rene was, his eyes lit up with pleasure.

'Oh ho,' he said. 'I remember you as a baby. When you were about three, you had snatched a piece of fried fish from my lunch thali and had run away! Do you remember? No, no, of course you don't. You were only a small bachcha.' Ramu could not seem to take his eyes off her.

Jai said sotto voce, 'She's been in the habit of running away with all kinds of stuff in her childhood, with my bike, for example.'

Nani asked Ramu to make some tea. His entry had given her the time she had needed to think about how she was going to break the news about Nimesh to Rene.

'Dimpy,' she said, after Ramu had walked reluctantly into the kitchen, 'I was thinking of a nice way to tell you this. But there isn't. Your brother, as he was born, does not exist anymore. Nimesh left home when he was barely a teenager, when he was about fourteen. He left in order to live the life of a woman, which is what he felt he was. She paused as her voice broke. He was, as he says in his poem, a girl trapped in a boy's body. He had begun to call himself Nimesha even as a child. See how he has crossed out the 'A' in the name? Just in case someone saw it, I suspect.'

****

CHAPTER 10

A Nightmare can be Real

Rene could only stare at Nani in shock. Her cheeks felt hot. This was too fantastic to be true. She thought of the book on the train, and again in the store; her dreams. But how had she *known*? Thoughts flew like sharp arrows through her head, stinging in their urgency. He – or rather she, was alive! She had hardly got used to the fact that she had had a brother, and was having to face the possibility that he was not a brother but a sister. Who had been a brother! Where was he, no – she? Why had he left? Why had he not gone to Australia with them?

'But where is he, Nani? Has no one ever tried to find him? Surely Dad and Mom must have? Surely, they wouldn't have left for Australia if he were still alive? It would have been, let's see, only about one year after he left home that we migrated to Sydney!'

Every question freshened the pain in Nani's heart, the pain that she had thought she had locked away. She answered,

'He is alive, child. Or that is what I pray for. Though if my guess is right, the life circumstances have forced him to live is no life, I can assure you. Our society is very intolerant of people like Nimesh. There is usually only one haven, if you can call it that, for such a one. He or she is probably living as what is known as a hijra, here in India. You live in a different land, my child; you can have no conception of who they are and how they live.'

'I know what a hijra is, Nani. It is not shocking to me that my brother has decided he wants to be one. I live in a culture where people live openly as gays and I know vaguely what a transgender is.

I can imagine, though, that most people are intolerant of anyone who is different. One of my friends in Uni was a lesbian. I had known her all my life, and it came as a shock when she told us. The discovery had traumatised her mother greatly. So much so, she did not see her daughter's pain when she asked her only child to move out of the family home. Only when my friend tried to kill herself with sleeping pills did her mother realise that she needed to accept her child for who she was, rather than see her die. There are many whom I know, Nani, workmates, acquaintances, many of whom are quite intolerant of anyone who does not conform to their idea of normal. But it is only now that I have heard about hijras and I have never met or known anyone who quite fits that description.'

Rene put her head in her hands. 'I just find it absurd that mum and dad kept all this from me. That I have spent nearly twenty-five years of my life not knowing that I have a sibling!' she said in a voice echoing with her frustration and confusion.

Jai came to where she was sitting and perched on the arm of her chair. Lightly touching her shoulder, he said,

'It is an awful lot to take in, and so suddenly. I wondered whether you remembered him at all. I remember him as a quiet sort of boy and I had known that there was some mystery surrounding his disappearance. But when we tried to ask our parents, they used to just shush us and wave us away. Though frankly, after all this time we had forgotten him and he had seemed almost like a figment of our imagination.'

Rene drew strength from his closeness. She looked at Nani and said, 'Please tell me everything, Nani. How...how did my brother come to be this way? Was he born intersexed or was he born male and did not develop at puberty? Or what?'

Both Nani and Jai looked at her in surprise. Most people in their circle had very little actual knowledge about the hijras. They seriously doubted that many people in their country had, other than those in the medical profession, if that. There seemed to be a shroud of mystery surrounding their origins and their physical characteristics. All Nani and Jai had seen of them was when they came to sing and dance at weddings, or when they had come to someone's house where a child had been born. In recent times, sometimes they had seen the hijras come to sing and dance even when a neighbour bought or built a new house. Most couples had fewer children these days, and the hijras needed to augment their income.

To most onlookers, they were men dressed as women, wearing saris and loud make up. To many, they were simply a nuisance, pestering people for money and clothes with ridiculous dances and mostly off-key melodies, until people were forced to pay them for their performance. Sometimes, they would resort to threatening to disrobe and show their private parts if someone did not pay, or did not pay enough. In Nani's opinion, very few people gave willingly in a genuine belief that a hijra's blessing would bring fertility and abundance or that their curse would be catastrophic. Most considered it as extortion. A few sincerely believed that a hijra's blessing would bring good fortune. Jai himself had very vague notions about them. He had thought that they were probably hermaphrodites or with ambiguous sexual anatomy. Or that they were men who were homosexuals, impotent or infertile, maybe. Vaguely, he had heard that a man went through castration to become a hijra. In truth, he told himself now, he hadn't given it a lot of thought. And as Rene herself said, there were no exact comparisons in the Western world.

So it was with astonishment that they heard Rene talk so knowledgably about them. Rene understood their surprise.

'This is going to appear totally incredible to you,' she said. 'It has been to me until now.' She told them about her nightmares, the recent 'encounters' with the term hijra that had fueled her curiosity into finding out about who they were and finally about her accidental discovery that she had had a brother.

'Now, though, it doesn't seem nearly so incredible anymore. I must have known Nimesh, and my dreams are recollections of those memories. They have to be! From his birth certificate, it appears that he was about seven years older than I was. At what age did he leave home, Nani? Do you know why?'

Nani wished she could spare Rene the pain she knew she would feel at what she was going to have to tell her. She did not want to tarnish the memories Rene had of her parents. Memories were all that the poor child had of them. But she knew that there was no way out of it now. Nani took her granddaughter's hands in hers and said,

'Nimesh left when he was fourteen. You were nearly seven years old. Physically, there was nothing ambiguous about him. I don't know what intersexed is, but if you mean he had both, um, organs, then no,' she said, looking embarrassed.

'He was born male. At fourteen you don't see children, you know, without clothes,' Nani shrugged. 'But the changes in the face and voice had started. So, I think he was developing in the normal way at puberty.'

'But,' she paused and seemed to look at a picture in the distance. 'Everything else about Nimesh was different from any boy I had ever known,' she continued. 'He had loved to dance since he had been a toddler. Not the boyish rough shuff type, but the graceful styles favoured by classical dancers or the type of dancing they performed in old movies, you know? He would see some film and come back and try to copy the steps in front of the mirror.

It was very amusing when he was little. But when he was ten, it began worrying his parents. Especially when he took to singing mainly female oriented songs and struck feminine poses copied from films in front of the mirror. And he sang beautifully too. He had such a melodious voice!

He went secretly to the Rabindra Bhavan Academy nearby. It was a school of dance and music close to your parents' house, where he watched girls learning to dance. Watched and learnt. Till one day, the mother of one girl who knew Deepa, your mother, came and told her.

"What is your son doing coming and watching girls dancing at this young age? Keep him in your control, otherwise he will become a roadside Romeo, mark my words!" she told Deepa, putting a totally different connotation on things.

When they found him practicing in his room in clothes borrowed from the maid's daughter, your parents could not delude themselves any longer. They had to face the fact that Nimesh was not a normal boy. That he was, in fact, a girl trapped in a boy's body.

Deepa and Naren may have dealt with the situation in a better way if your Dadi hadn't come to live with you just about that time. She was intensely curious and an interfering busybody. She listened at doors and questioned servants. Within a short time, she found out that something was not quite right with Nimesh. She found his knitting, his dolls. Within days, she had turned the household upside down with her rantings and ravings. She yelled at Deepa,

"Yeh hijra banega kya?" Will he become a hijra?' Nani translated. 'Your Dadi ranted on,

"Playing with dolls! Wearing the ayah's frock! He will cause our nose to be cut' – meaning that he would bring them humiliation. "Why did you not tell me all this before?" she asked your father.

It was no surprise that she blamed your mother, saying that it was *her* fault for not sorting him out from the beginning with a good old walloping. All this was in Nimesh's hearing. Also, in the servants' hearing! Deepa tried to calm her down, but it only made your Dadi's rantings worse. She had never accepted the fact that your father had married your mother in a love marriage. A girl from his college and not one that she had chosen for him! And what was worse, a girl from a lower caste than their own. In her bigoted mind, her caste and Nimesh's behaviour were somehow connected. Anyhow, whatever she really thought, she got the fresh ammunition she needed to make your mother suffer even more. Your mother, by this time, was quietly slipping over the edge.

I think it was this that Nimesh could not bear. Seeing his beloved mother suffer because of him. One day, he just ran away. He took nothing except the money from his piggy bank, some clothes and his school satchel.'

'But what about dad? Where was he in all this? Why didn't *he* do something about all that was happening?' Rene's face was pinched from the sadness of it all.

'I think he couldn't deal with his mother. He was weak. And he was frightened too of the humiliation he and his family would face in society along with Nimesh,' said Nani. 'You were just seven years old. If people outside the family came to know, as they surely would, your chances of growing up unaffected by it all would not exist. Perhaps he thought no one would have married you later. They would have shunned Nimesh for sure. But maybe, he would have tried to hide things for as long as he could or leave the country with everyone – as he finally did, if your Dadi hadn't let the cat out of the bag. One night, she was screaming at Nimesh,

'Tu hijra hai, hijra, hijra, hijra.' She had discovered him in his room, dancing like a girl in front of the mirror, wearing one of your mother's sarees.'

Rene stared. She now realised why she had had that sense of deja vu that day on the train, as if she had seen and heard all this before. It was suddenly all falling into place. And it hit her then that she *must* have heard the screams. The boy being shaken; herself cowering at the door, looking on, terrified. That grey haired woman, her dad's mother! Those dreams, the screaming, were all very real now. A flash of memory showed a little girl standing at the door, watching a short, middle-aged woman screaming the word she hadn't forgotten – at an older girl. No, she now realised, at a boy dressed as a girl. Nimesh. Hijra!

A second thought followed closely on the first. This also probably explained her imaginary girlfriend. It must have been Nimesh, dressed as a girl!

Nani was speaking. 'When he ran away, your mother went to pieces. Your father searched for him everywhere but did not inform the police, thinking of the humiliation. I was extremely harsh to him about this, when I was finally told about what had occurred. I called him and said that he was less than a man. That Nimesh was more of one for having the courage to run away and thereby protect his mother from Dadi's harshness. Something *he* had not done. I am afraid I completely lost it when I saw the terrible state my daughter was in.

He finally contacted my son Rajan's friend, who was in the Delhi police. He made enquiries in Delhi, in slums, in hijra communities, but to no avail. Finally, he was advised that Nimesh could have gone anywhere. Someone reportedly saw a boy of his description buying a ticket to Varanasi. The police made enquiries there as well.

But the hijra community can be extremely secretive, and they know how to protect their own. If Nimesh did not want to be found, they would not find him. By that time, it was probably too late. He may have been castrated and become a *nirvaan*.'

'A nirvaan? What is that, Nani?' she asked.

Nani replied a little hesitantly, embarrassed to be speaking of what was normally a taboo topic. 'Nirvaan is a term given to those hijras who have been castrated. They are called nirvaan hijras, meaning that they have been released from their male gender and have been reborn.'

Castrated! Rene remembered what she had read on the train, in the book which had started this journey. She remembered that some hijras went through unhealthy and dangerous procedures like castration to make the transition irrevocable and shuddered at the mere thought.

****

CHAPTER 11

Nana

'Damyanti, who is there? Who are you talking to?' came a voice from within, followed by the speaker himself, a short, very thin man, who looked every bit of his eighty-year-old age. His carriage, though, was very upright, and the speed with which he covered the distance to the sofa on which Nani and Rene were sitting belied his age.

'And who is this pretty girl?' he asked as he took in Rene's appearance at a glance. 'Why Jai, have you finally taken the plunge? I know. I took one look at Damyanti and I was gone. What is your name, beta? You are so lovely, as lovely…. no,' he amended, 'almost as lovely as my Damyanti,' he grinned.

It would have been funny if it had not been so sad. There was embarrassment on Nani's face and a mischievous glint in Jai's eyes as he struggled not to laugh aloud. Nani said with faked annoyance,

'Looks like you have had a really satisfying siesta and still sleeping. Look closely and tell me you can't really tell *who* the child is.'

Nana's normally sharp brain failed him today. He was not good at playing who's who and who's whose.

'Go ahead, tell me. I know you are bursting to,' he said. When she did, he looked for a chair, which Jai promptly placed behind him and sat down. A suspicious shine appeared in the old man's eyes as he looked with a longing long suppressed at his granddaughter. Rene touched his feet as she had seen Jai do and was immediately enfolded in a surprisingly powerful bear hug.

'My own grandchild and I could not know you! And the spitting image of my Damyanti. Sit here next to me,' he said, moving to a settee by the window, 'and tell me everything about you, *beta*.'

In between sipping tea and eating the hot spinach pakoras that Ramu had made, the story was told again. Nana seemed to be lost in thought. Suddenly, he turned to Nani.

'I was thinking, Damyanti, won't Rajan be able to help? He is in the police, after all.'

'I was thinking along the same lines, but you know Sudha. She may not take kindly to raking up the past. Even though we had told her parents everything before the wedding, Sudha prefers to pretend that Nimesh never existed. She is not a very accommodating person, as you very well know. But of course, we can ask and hope that Rajan can at least suggest what we can do to find Nimesh,' Nani said.

'Rajan is your *mama*, child, your mother's only sibling,' explained Nani as Rene looked at them, a frown puzzling her brow. 'I can't pretend that Sudha, his wife, is very easy to get along with. She has very bigoted notions about everything. Things are black or white. She is a Brahmin and looks down on every other caste. In this day and age! There, I am talking like a typical mother-in-law! But it's true that everything bothers Sudha in the extreme. Except, of course, Rajan's boss, the commissioner of police and his wife, who she sucks up to big time even though he is not a Brahmin,' said Nani, chuckling.

Nana looked out at the darkening winter sky and announced that it was time for his evening walk and that if the youngsters wanted, they could come along. Jai immediately stood up and looked at Rene.

'It would be great to stretch my legs a little. Want to come?' he queried.

Nani urged Rene to go, thinking it would give her a bit of time to assimilate all that she had learnt today.

Rene got up promptly to go out with the two men and looked around with pleasure at the narrow lanes and charming cottages bursting with pink and blue hydrangeas, bougainvillea and some flowers she could not name. Nana looked at them strolling and said,

'You call this walking? Meet me at the roundabout near the Mall. I need to *walk*!' Soon he was a speck in the distance, walking quickly, amazingly sprightly for his age.

Jai draped a casual arm around her shoulders.

'At the risk of stating the obvious,' he said, 'you really have had a huge shock today. I mean, I am in shock myself and I am not even connected in the way that you are. Do you want to stay the night or a couple? I haven't anything major happening which I can't delegate, so it's okay with me. Also, as I had mentioned to you earlier, I wanted to catch up with an old teacher who lives in Sanawar, just a short drive from here. Would you like to see the place as well? It's really beautiful and you might as well see something of it while you are here.'

Rene felt overwhelmed at his perception and kindness. She nodded her agreement and, shortly afterwards, they caught up with Nana, who was sitting on a round, concrete bench built around a sprawling banyan tree. He was eating what looked like doughnuts and some orange coloured, spiral shaped sweet. Beside him on the bench was a glass of steaming tea, sending out an aroma of ginger and cardamom.

'*Jalebis*! I love them!' Rene could not keep herself from taking one of the sweet, juicy spirals as Nana held out the plate. She refused the doughnut like thing, which Jai assured her was not a doughnut at all but a fried savoury snack called a *vada*. He found he enjoyed teasing her about her lack of knowledge of things Indian, things he took for granted.

'I know what a *vada* is, Mr. Indian, but I had never seen one with a hole in it,' Rene laughed.

On the way back, Nana swore them to secrecy about the *jalebis* and the *vadas* because Nani would have a fit if she knew.

'She controls my sugar intake, you see, and keeps telling me that Ramu makes great vadas. But what is the fun in having home made things, hmm? The road side ones always taste better. She even tries to fool me by putting home-made vadas in paper bags – to make me think they are store bought ones. As if I can't tell the difference!' And giving an innocent looking grin, he started walking again, this time at a slower pace, and chatted about things past, his daughter and his son, and his son's family living in Delhi. Jai saw Rene eagerly soaking up all the stories about the missing bits in her family's life and his heart went out to her.

Meanwhile, Nani had been busy. She had got Ramu to prepare the guest bedroom for Rene, taking it as a foregone conclusion that she would stay with them. Nani showed Rene to her room. Here too, like at Seema's grandmother's house, a white mosquito net hung over the bed, tied with strings to four hooks on the wall. The bed was an Indian double, bigger than even the king-sized beds in Sydney. She washed up and joined the rest for a dinner of chapatis, chickpea curry and salad. As Jai got up to go to his company guest house, Nani looked shocked.

'There is a divan bed right here which Ramu has made up for you. Stay. Why should you go all the way to your guest house?' 'All the way' was a mere ten minutes' drive, which for the residents of Kasauli was still too far away.

Rene asked Nani if she would mind if she went with Jai to see Sanawar and got mildly scolded for her pains.

'Go child. You will like the place. But I am hoping you will stay for a few days with me. We have so much to catch up on.'

Rene agreed to stay for two more days and Nani said she would visit her son in Delhi as soon as she could so that she could spend more time with her.

Nani came to see whether she was comfortably settled in bed, bringing a bottle of water for the night. She half lay as she stroked Rene's forehead with her hand, her touch evoking forgotten memories of her mother in Rene. A lump rose in her throat and without Rene saying anything, Nani understood her need to talk, or rather *hear*, about the mother that she had lost and the brother she had never known. Late into the night, Nani told Rene little known stories of her mother, sometimes funny, sometimes sad. She dared not share her own feeling of loss for her daughter with whom she had lost touch much before her death; or that Rene's father had asked her not to call because every time she spoke to her mother, Deepa became depressed, reminded as she was of her past and her son Nimesh.

****

CHAPTER 12

Sanawar

There had been a slight drizzle through the night, which cleared up by the time Rene had her shower in the morning. It took her some getting used to having a 'shower' from a bucket and a plastic jug. There was hot water from a geyser and Rene loved the sandalwood scent of the soap. As she walked into the dining room, she heard voices and saw that Jai and Nani were already on their second cup of coffee and tea, respectively. Jai's hair was still wet from his shower and he looked to Rene's eyes, good enough to eat! She tried to control the strange awareness she had of him this morning and failed.

'Good morning,' she said, and sat down next to Nani, after giving her a quick hug. 'My, this looks more like brunch,' she exclaimed on looking at the spread of toast, marmalade, cereal and steaming hot *idlis* with *sambar* that Ramu had made. Rene loved the steamed dumplings made with rice and white lentils, eating them with the sour savoury daal.

'Eat properly, beta,' said Nani. 'Ramu has prepared some sandwiches for your lunch in case you are not back from Sanawar by then. If they get soggy and you can get back by lunchtime, don't eat them. Take some water from the filter. Jai, don't let her eat roadside food.' A few more words of advice later, Nani was satisfied that it was safe to let Rene go for a less than fifteen minutes' drive to Sanawar.

The six-kilometre drive to Sanawar was achieved through a winding road climbing into the pine and deodar laden Sanawar Hills located at an altitude of 1750 metres. Soon, the red rooftops of The Lawrence School were visible from a long way before they reached the campus. The school grounds were breathtaking, spread over as they were on a hundred and thirty-nine acres. Fragrant conifers, lush green forests of cedar and oak made for a breathtaking sight. Jai was looking at her expectantly and she could see the boyish pride for his alma mater in his eyes.

He spoke to the guard at the huge scrolled iron gates and they drove through. Jai pointed out a few of the buildings, some more than a hundred years old, some even older, most with their brick walls and the ubiquitous red roofs. They parked near the administrative block, and entered a beautiful heritage building, its front walls hidden under masses of green creeper.

A man at the desk asked them to wait while he went inside to see if Jai's old teacher was available. A few minutes later, a very tall man with bushy hair peppered with grey and a short beard came out and greeted Jai and Rene. He fixed Rene with his penetrating grey eyes and, with an enigmatic look towards Jai, led them towards his office. Jai introduced him as his economics teacher, Om Dixit.

After a few minutes of reminiscing, they realised Rene might be feeling left out and Mr. Dixit turned to Rene and proceeded to embarrass Jai thoroughly by saying,

'You know, Rene Jai was one of my best students but also one of the laziest. He was always the last to wake up in the mornings.' He had also been a House Master in Jai's residential block. They had tea and cake and as they rose to take his leave, Jai took out an envelope from the pocket of his jacket and handed it over to his teacher.

'Please give this to the Princi, he said with a twinkle. I was coming over, so I thought I would just hand it to him instead of posting it. I thought I would just show Rene around the school and my old Res building since we are here.'

'Ah, your donation cheque! You really are very generous, Jai. Yes, yes, please show Rene around the grounds. Make the most of your visit. Don't forget to show her the cathedral, Jai. Although, somehow, I have a feeling that we will be seeing this young lady again, and soon, eh, son?' he said, with his eyebrows raised at Jai.

Jai led Rene outside and showed her the school chapel with its lovely stained glass windows, as promised. They drove over to the residential blocks and he showed her the one called Himalayas, the one in which he had spent his senior years. A tour of the cricket and playing fields followed. Just before leaving, Jai took her to his favourite relaxation place, a small outcrop of rock at the end of a path lined with old oaks, from where the view of the Himalayas was as beautiful as it was peaceful.

****

As the peace and beauty of the surrounding Shivalik Hills settled upon Rene, the enormity of all that she had learned the day before kicked in, and she found to her dismay that she was crying. Being the perceptive man that he was, Jai did not need any words of explanation. He hesitated and then with a muttered 'what the hell,' he gathered her in his arms and let her cry till she seemed to quieten and become still.

'I'm sorry,' said Rene, 'I kind of lost it. And now your shirt is all wet.'

'It has all been a bit too much for you sweetheart, don't worry about my shirt. I have a kerchief around somewhere. Here.' He wiped a tear which had escaped to her chin with his thumb and drew her closer. When she looked up, it took all his self-control not to kiss her there and then. He did not know then that it was exactly what Rene was trying to do. For the moment, though, she satisfied herself by burrowing as close to him as she dared.

A bird flew out suddenly from one of the highest hills and Jai reluctantly let Rene go as they turned towards the paved path to return to the car. Rene felt better as they drove out of the school grounds in companionable silence.

'Would you like to do some of the touristy stuff? There is Monkey Point which is niceish. Hanuman, you know the monkey God, was supposed to have touched the top of the hill with his foot. And the Mall has shops if you want some mementoes. And,' he added, his expression leery, 'There is Lover's Lane for a nice ahem, walk. Lots of pleasant walks around here, actually.'

Rene did not want to go back just yet, so they went to Monkey Point. They climbed up to the little temple there and looked at the Sutlej River flowing serenely below. In the distance, Jai pointed out the direction of the city of Chandigarh to her. They ended up going to Lover's Lane as well, which turned out to be a narrow, cobbled path with chest wood trees lined on both sides. It was charming; with breathtaking views of the town and the surrounding snow covered Himalayan peaks. There seemed to be some serious bird watchers with their cameras and Rene could see why when Jai pointed out some rare and exotic looking birds to her from time to time.

****

It seemed only natural to walk hand in hand from there to the unmetalled Gilbert Trail, which was as lovely as it was intimate. Rene was very conscious of her hand in Jai's and found it strange that she was so attracted to him after having known him for such a short time. She smiled to herself as she thought of Seema's and Helen's reaction if they knew.

'What's so funny?' asked the object of her rumination. He was looking at her with a smile of his own and Rene said without thinking,

'I was just wondering what my friends' reaction to us would be. They are always trying to get me fixed with some guy or the other.'

'Oh, is there an *us*? Even if there isn't, we could *make* an us. We are not far away from Scandal Point, you know. In any case,' he murmured softly, 'I can't stand it anymore Rene.' As he spoke, he took her in his arms under a strategically placed giant oak and kissed her with a barely masked urgency. 'God, you're so lovely. And charming. And you've been driving me crazy for the last couple of days.'

Rene was shocked at her response to Jai. She found that she wanted him to stop talking, to not stop kissing her. *I hardly know him, for God's sake.* She had known him when she was a child, but that didn't count. He felt her response, and he realised as he looked around and saw the shocked or amused glances of passersby, how out of control he was, like a schoolboy in fact. He did not remember reacting like this to anyone in a long time. None of his woman friends in all his adult life had had the effect that this woman was having on him in a few short days. It was not just that she was beautiful. There was something so fresh and unpretentious about her. The way she spoke, the way she smiled, her sense of humour. It was also the vulnerability he sensed in her, but more than anything, he admired her spirit. It drew him to her like a magnet. He felt protective; he thought she would slap him down if he tried to be so.

Get a hold on yourself, man, he told himself. This was not going anywhere. Rene would return to Australia when she had done what she had come to India to do, and that would be that.

They sat under the oak tree and ate the sandwiches that Nani had packed for them. Jai pulled her up, and they returned to Nani's house just as she was getting down from a rickshaw laden with bags of groceries.

'I always shop for the vegetables myself. I can never remember what to ask Ramu to get, so I get what I see and like.' she told them. Jai and Rene helped carry the bags indoors, and as they put them away, Nani asked and received an abridged version of how they had spent the day. She took out some rice pudding she had made while they had been out and served them in small steel bowls.

'I remembered suddenly that you used to love to eat *kheer* as a child, in fact, anything sweet. I was not sure that you liked it still, but I made some. Do try it.' Nani smiled, seeing Rene's eyes light up.

'*Kheer*! Of course! I still love it, only I haven't had it in years! Seema's Dadi made something similar, with vermicelli in Delhi. I love pudding of any kind. Back home, I make do with sago pudding and kulfi. We get cashew *barfi* in Sydney but I have lost the taste for the syrupy Indian sweets. Except jalebis of course!'

'The kheer is lovely. Could I have some more, please? Just a tiny bit, thanks.' Out of the corner of her eye, she saw Jai filling up his bowl again and in two minutes, had finished it all again.

'Thou of evil eye, thy face is black,' Jai said when he realised she was watching him wolf down the kheer. They both burst into peals of laughter, with Nani joining in even though she did not know what the joke was. Jai told her about the trucks and their messages and, even though she rolled her eyes at them, she smiled indulgently. It warmed her to see her granddaughter happy and laughing.

****

CHAPTER 13

Bonding

Rene was conscious of Jai like never before. She felt herself go warm with pleasure every time he looked at her, and she felt sure Nani would sense the change in her. But, to her comfort, Nani did not know her well enough and at the best of times was as absent minded as they come. Helen and Seema would have sensed something in a moment. That thought chased another. She had not written to them after coming to Kasauli. In fact, not since she had met Jai. When she asked Nani whether she could use her computer, Jai offered her his laptop.

As she sat in the little sun room looking out at a pretty back yard and checked her mail, Jai was getting a conducted tour of the garden. Nani had a cottage garden of sorts, full of herbs and fragrant shrubs which were favoured by the Kasauli climate. She pointed out some to Jai and gathered some fresh salad greens and an assortment of herbs.

Meanwhile, Rene was well on her way to bringing her two best friends up to date with her journey so far, thus:

Hi girls,

I know, I know. I meant to write earlier, but I have been travelling. A lot has happened in the meantime and it is very hard to find the words to describe what I have since discovered about my brother, rather, my sister. Confused? I am not sure I can describe what I am feeling!

Let me start with the good part. I found my grandparents, mum's parents. They are alive and are such lovely people. I believe I also have two uncles and aunts *and* cousins. I feel that a huge part of what has been missing in my life has suddenly been found and fulfilled. Nimesh or Nimesha, as she probably calls herself, is alive; at least that is what I desperately hope. He was born a boy, but discovered when he was very young that he really was a female trapped in a boy's body. My brother is really my sister now!

Now the bad part. He ran away when he was fourteen. No one knows where he is. He could be anywhere. Maybe not even alive. Nani thinks that the likelihood of him living in a transgender community has the highest probability. But there are so many communities out there! He could be in any city in India, and I don't have the foggiest idea of how to even begin looking for her. See, I don't even know whether to refer to Nimesh as him or her! Nana thinks that mum's brother (whom BTW I didn't know existed and whom I haven't seen since I was a child) may be able to help. I will know once I get back to Delhi in a couple of days. Jai is also going to ask his dad if he can help look for Nimesha. He, Jai's dad, is a retired police commissioner or something and has a network of police buddies in many of the cities.

Jai has been awesome! If it hadn't been for his support, I think I would have caved in by now. Oh yes, I haven't mentioned Jai before, have I? He is the 'cousin' who has been helping me find my grandparents and has come with me to Kasauli to see them. He is staying here too and insists on driving back with me. He is really amazing. A very helpful guy and so perceptive and witty. I went with him to see his old school yesterday. You could probably build ten more private schools on the grounds; they are so extensive! Nice, colonial kind of architecture. Jai is the founder and CEO of a few companies, but isn't one of the tall poppies, though. I had thought with his looks and wealth (and women chasing him) he must be the spoilt, charmer variety, but he is quite the opposite. It's weird the way I have begun to rely on Jai, even though I have known him only a few days (my childhood doesn't really count.) He is sensitive and helpful without being in your face. Know what I mean?

I so wish you two could be here with me. I miss you guys terribly. What's happening with the wedding dates, Seema? Did you get the place you wanted? Write soon, you two. I need to be kept sane. Love you lots.

Cheers, Rene.

She shut down the computer and walked out into the garden and gazed at the two still pottering about in the backyard. Rene soon realised that she was staring at Jai and glanced away. *What was happening to her?* I am behaving like a high school girl with a crush on a senior. She caught up with them just as Jai was saying,

'I see you've got Nasturtiums. Let me make the salad Nani. I'll put some of these in. I am quite handy in the kitchen, so don't look at me like that.'

****

While Jai was making some calls to his office, Nani took Rene to her 'studio,' as she called her renovated garage. As she entered, a mixture of beautiful fragrances assailed Rene and her nose twitched with pleasure. She soon saw the reason for the smells. A variety of herbs were drying in the small room, which had glass French windows on two sides, letting the afternoon sun in. Here and there, rosemary and lavender hung in bunches from the rafters of the slanting roof. Tables were laden with sage, thyme, basil and other herbs that she could not identify.

Nani had climbed what Rene thought was a very precarious looking ladder; to tie some more of the fresh bunches of lavender she had gathered from the garden. She got down and pointed out Neem to Rene. Rene picked up a jar full of dry rose petals and another of some herb infusing in what looked like oil.

'What a beautiful room, what lovely smells! But what are they for, Nani?'

Nani chuckled, 'This is my secret life, beta, started not so many years ago. I use these herbs to make soaps, lotions and infused oils. At first, it was just a hobby. But now I send them to Delhi for the craft market at Dilli Bazaar and to a couple of local shops here in Kasauli. A tourist who I met some years ago gave me the idea of turning my hobby into a business. She came home for tea, saw what I was doing, and offered to market them for me. I don't get much of a profit but, at least my hobby pays for itself.'

'Oh, how fantastic!' exclaimed Rene. 'Some of these soaps look good enough to eat!'

'I'll pack some for you Dimpy. These rose geranium ones here have been curing for almost six weeks and are ready.'

'I would love some Nani. I keep buying handmade soaps at our craft markets. But you must let me pay you for them,' said Rene. Nani looked aghast, as if she had said the most scandalizing thing in the world.

'Child, I am your grandmother, and I will take *money* from you?' She looked slightly hurt. Rene put her arms around her and said,

'I'm sorry Nani, I'll take all your stock and won't pay, okay?' And she was glad to see her smile again. It felt strange that she had grown so attached to her grandmother in such a short while.

They walked into the kitchen together and both of them were taken aback to see Jai there already, putting the finishing touches to a salad. He looked such a hilarious sight with Nani's brightly coloured flower print apron on. He turned to a pot on the stove and was busy stirring it despite the protests of a very harassed looking Ramu.

'Someone sure is talented,' said Rene, trying unsuccessfully to take a peek into the pot. He put his hands on her shoulders and gently marched her into the sitting room. The touch of Jai's hands on her shoulders sent a shiver down her body and she was shocked at how strongly she felt like turning into his arms there and then, despite Nani's presence in the room.

Jai asked both her and Nani to wait in the sitting room or do whatever except enter his kitchen. Nani and Rene both raised their eyebrows and tried to stop from bursting into laughter, but couldn't help themselves.

'*His* kitchen,' said Nani, and they both giggled like teenagers. Jai put on a mock hurt expression, muttered something under his breath and walked back to the kitchen. Dinner was worth the wait though, as Jai had made a delicious stew of chicken and vegetables with some secret herbs, which he refused to divulge until they had eaten and praised his cooking. The salad was unusual too, and Nana also ate with gusto.

****

CHAPTER 14

Strange Feelings

In the late evening, they all went for a walk in the Lower Mall and wandered into some of the shops. In one of them, Rene bought a pretty paisley patterned shawl for Nani in spite of her protests and some earrings for the girls back home. She wanted to buy something for Jai, but thought it was too soon. She checked herself. *Too soon for what?* There was not going to be any *later*. Rene shook her head at herself and entered one of the colourful looking shops selling clothes, bags, shoes, all the wares taking up almost half of the road space. She bought a scarf for herself, a bag for Dadi and gifts for her uncle, aunt and their two daughters and came back to where the rest of them were waiting.

When Jai and Rene said they wanted to go on to the Upper Mall, Nani begged off and went back home while Nana took off for his own 'real' walk, as he called it. Jai and Rene walked up and were glad that here at least cars were not allowed to come. They saw a sign on the way saying:

Singapore – fine for littering = clean countryside

India – No fine = clogged with litter

Kasauli – you pay rupees 2,500 for littering, so beware!

The two laughed and made their way up the slightly winding road.

The Upper Mall was very pretty, with its winding cobbled street and lovely views. They wandered through a gate set into stone walls and, after walking for a few minutes, sat on a stone seat looking out at the sunset over the mountains. It seemed very natural for Jai to put his arms around her and kiss her as if that was exactly what she wanted. Rene decided she would not think about later and gave herself to the moment. They stayed snuggled together until Jai looked at the darkening sky and they made their way back home.

As Rene walked back with her hand held tightly in Jai's, she felt she was walking in the clouds and suddenly realised why. The mist forming in the night was low enough to touch the top of her head, and her hair felt slightly damp. She could barely see Jai's face, as it was almost lost in the mist. It sort of brought home to her that she really knew very little about him. The shock of all that she had learned in the last few days made that somehow unimportant. They made their way back to her grandparents' house without any mishap.

****

Nani had a pot of tea ready and they played a game of Snakes and Ladders, in which Nana refused to join. He joined them later for a card game called twenty-nine, needing four people. Nana showed Rene how to play the game. She had Nani were partners and Rene enjoyed it immensely, more because of the togetherness.

'You should have seen how my grandmother, God rest her soul, used to cheat at the game. She used facial signs like putting out her tongue or winking to hint at the suit picked, until the entire family knew the 'rules' of cheating, everyone in the family having partnered her at various times,' Jai said, his description making everyone laugh uproariously.

The next day, Nani took Rene to the local markets, where she had a stall for her soaps and creams. Rene enjoyed being introduced to the locals, who stopped by and remained chatting with Nani and herself. They were openly curious about her and her sudden appearance after so many years. Some of the other stall holders also chatted with her and Nani's regular customers asked whether she would come to the markets every week with Nani.

When Rene remarked to Nani how she seemed to enjoy being at the markets, Nani explained that she had had to go through what was almost a rite of passage to be taken seriously by the people there.

'The first time, people would just check you out, the second maybe buy something, maybe not, but they would expect to find you there. Only after the third week they would accept you as one of their own and as a firmly entrenched member. It keeps me busy and engaged with the community here, and time just passes with the many friends I have made here,' she said.

****

Soon, too soon, it seemed to both Nani and Rene; it was time to head back to Delhi. Nana made the necessary call to his son Rajan that his niece Tarini was here from Australia and why. He asked Rajan to help her out in any way he could. Rajan understood from those softly spoken words that he must do it. It was extremely rare for his father to ask him something. In fact, he could scarcely remember such an occasion after he had become an adult. He understood that there was no scope for him to refuse.

From somewhere to his right Sudha, his wife whispered that there was no spare room or bed in their house. He said as much to Nani when she spoke to him and added that he would make arrangements for her stay in a lodge nearby. Nani said,

'That will not be necessary, dear, as Rene is staying with the Naithanis. If you can help with the search and transport if she needs it, that would be more than enough.'

****

Rene and Jai set off on a drizzly morning on their way back to Delhi. Jai seemed thoughtful on the journey back. When he thought she wasn't looking, he kept giving Rene sidelong glances.

Once or twice, he pointed out an interesting or funny truck saying, but did not entertain her with any of his usual jokes. They ate at a restaurant on the way back where Rene asked for butter chicken and was surprised when the waiter told her it wasn't on the menu.

'It isn't that common to find that in restaurants here, you know,' was Jai's response to her query.

'Oh, that's strange because no self-respecting Indian restaurant in Sydney would be caught without butter chicken on the menu. Oh well, I'll have the lamb *rogan josh* instead and naan, please.'

Rene wondered at Jai's preoccupation. She thought maybe that he was already regretting what had happened between them. Maybe he was not the commitment type. Commitment type? What was she thinking? Commitment to what? Herself? *Where* was she going with all this? Hold on! She checked herself. She had her home and work in Sydney to get back to as soon as she had found Nimesha. If she found her, that is.

Manju Dadi was glad to see her back. She was bursting with curiosity and full of questions for Rene. She asked Jai to stay for dinner, but he declined, saying that he had some papers to go through before going to work the next day.

****

Over dinner of chapatti, okra and daal, Rene filled in Dadi with all that she had learnt about Nimesh from her grandparents. Dadi was aghast at all that she heard. Her eyes filled with tears at the sadness of it all, and she did not mince words when she spoke angrily about Rene's Dadi. She placed her hand on Rene's and said,

'I hope you can ultimately find your brother, beta. But I am not sure whether you will like what you find. Who knows whether he will want to meet you? Your lives have been so very different. Different experiences, different countries. He may even resent you for what you have, you know.'

'Do you think I haven't thought about that, Dadi? It is constantly on my mind. But I have still got to do it, let the consequences be whatever. And hope for the best,' Rene replied and prayed in her heart that it would indeed be for the best.

Rene went to bed thinking that she would be meeting yet another of her lost relatives in the morning. It was her uncle Rajan's day off and he had invited her to spend the day at his house in Greater Kailash.

****

CHAPTER 15

An Uncle and an Aunt

A stark white portly Ambassador car, with a police beacon on top, stood outside the gates of Dadi's house the next morning. As soon as the gates opened and Rene walked out, a man in a khaki uniform got out from the driver's seat and saluted her smartly. Rene was taken aback. But she quietened her astonishment by telling herself that it was probably a done thing. She was getting quite good at accepting a lot of *done things* in India these days. For instance, she did not blink once when the driver opened the door at the back for her to sit instead of wondering why he did not require her to sit in front. So she simply nodded and smiled and got into the back seat of the car. She thought to herself as she did so that she would be rendered quite useless at doing things for herself if she stayed here very long. But oh, for a chauffeur driven car in Sydney! A wishful thought as she sank back into the plump seats, covered with a white toweling type material.

The drive to her uncle's house was not far, but it took them more than half an hour because of the teeming traffic. On the way, they passed what looked like a temple on the top of a hill. Tiny orange flags led the way up the path. When she asked the driver, who was actually a police constable, he explained that it was a very famous temple called Kalkaji Mandir. At certain times of the year, the thronging devotees would block off the road completely, he added. They drove past what seemed to be an office precinct called Nehru Place before they entered the very busy looking suburb of Greater Kailash.

They stopped before a very modern looking double storeyed house painted a pleasant cream and chocolate brown. A guard in police uniform opened the grilled gates of a matching brown. He saluted smartly as Rene got out of the car. A short, plump woman came out on the first-floor balcony, smiled and disappeared, only to reappear again at the front door.

Sudha, uncle Rajan's wife, was dressed as if she was going out, in a pretty pink and blue tie and dye saree, with earrings and bangles to match. A very thin, tall woman, possibly in her mid-fifties, her eyes deep with curiosity, followed her. The laughter lines around her eyes and mouth told of a lady with a sense of humour. She was dressed elegantly in a Bengal handloom sari and a diamond stud twinkled on her small, pert nose. Rene hoped she did not look underdressed in her ubiquitous kurta and jeans. She was bending to touch her *mami's* feet when Sudha caught her by the shoulders and said,

'There is no need for all that, child. Please come in. Leave your shoes outside, yes, just there is fine. You look so much like Mummyji, your Nani, you know. My younger daughter Shweta also looks a lot like her. They, that is, both my daughters are out. Shweta is at school. She is in class twelve and Naina is at work. But you will see them in the evening. Sit, sit, I will call your uncle. Oh, and this is your bua, Yamini didi.' She got all that out in a rush, as if she had rehearsed it all morning.

Uncle Rajan came into the living room at that instant. He was the spitting image of his father, right down to his twinkling eyes. Rene took to him immediately; although he did not look at all like her mother, he reminded Rene of her somehow. Was her sadness reflected in his eyes? He enveloped her in a bear hug, if you could call a hug from a tall slim man that. In a crisp white kurta pajama embroidered in Lucknow Chikan work, Uncle Rajan looked very elegant. He straightened and looked at her, holding her at arm's length.

'I heard what Sudha said. You *do* look just like Ma, you know. The very image of this picture here.' He pointed at a framed photograph hanging on the wall amidst many other family photographs. They were interrupted by a young boy of about twelve or thirteen who came in with a tray laden with steaming hot tea, samosas, and a plate of the mouth-watering *jalebis*. The cups were tiny, more like those in her play tea set that she had had as a child. Rene ate one of the *jalebis* but avoided the samosas, not sure whether her stomach would be up to them.

They chatted about life in Australia and her mother's childhood but did not venture into the topic that Rene was really here to talk about. Rene noticed that when Sudha spoke in Hindi, she used the respectful pronoun in referring to her husband and did not take his name at all.

Rene took out the presents that she had brought from Kasauli and as she handed them to her aunt and uncle, she said,

'I could not bring anything from home, as I didn't know I would be meeting you here. I hope you like these.'

'Oh, we get everything here in India these days,' said Sudha smugly. 'Gone are the days when people used to crave for foreign things in India, you know. We have lots of malls now. We get everything, everything,' she finished.

'I don't think Dimpy meant it in quite that way, Sudha. You always go out of context in your responses,' intervened Rajan gently while Yamini only smiled and rolled her eyes heavenwards. That was usually Rajan's way with his wife. He had understood quite early in his marriage that apart from being pretty and being an excellent housekeeper, Sudha did not have much to offer to their relationship. In fact, for the most part, he found her a very trying woman to live with. She was very superficial and extremely defensive in most of her relationships. So, he treated her comments with gentle ridicule, if not outright disdain. That was the only way he could tolerate her silliness.

'They are lovely, thank you, child. I am sure your cousins will be delighted with their presents. Please have some more of the snacks,' Rajan offered.

Rene asked for childhood pictures of her mum and Sudha brought out some old albums. Rene spent a good hour poring over them. Eagerly, she soaked in every anecdote or incident concerning her mother and her brother, while Yamini bua looked on indulgently.

On her way to the bathroom to wash her hands before lunch, Rene heard her name mentioned and heard Sudha mami say in an agitated voice,

'We have a position in society. You need to think about your position too, you know. After all, you are a superintendent of police. What will people say if they come to know? At least think about your daughters! How will it affect their chances of marriage if people come to know about your nephew? I don't think you should involve yourself in all this! I have said what I feel! Now it is your wish!'

'Position, position! That's all you ever think about! In any case, I would only be helping to find my sister's child. I should have done something about that a long time ago. Maybe my sister would not have died of heartache then. God has given us a chance to help. After all these years, this child has come to us seeking help, and it is the least I can do. Try to think with your heart instead of thinking of your own interests for once.' Rene decided to step in at that point and said gently,

'I am sorry mami, I heard you both talking from the hallway. See Rajan uncle, please don't stress about this. I would be very grateful for your help for sure. However, if it's going to create problems of any kind for *any* of you, I would rather you didn't. And don't worry, I totally understand. Of course, if you can help, nobody need know that I am related to you or that you are trying to trace someone related to you, do they? I would be happy if you can just point me in the right direction or give me some contacts that could be of help.'

Sudha had the grace to look ashamed at showing her meanness so patently. Rajan, however, put his arm around her shoulders and said,

'Don't worry beta, I will do my best to find Nimesh and for your sake Sudha, I will not mention to anyone that we are looking for a relative, if that makes you feel easier.'

Somewhat mollified, Sudha offered to take Rene to the nearby M Block market after lunch. It was an affluent neighbourhood, and the market was definitely for the seriously well heeled. Rene's eyes popped out at some of the price tags in one shop and she said as much to Sudha. She was told that it was owned by a well-known designer and took Rene to some of the other boutiques, where she shopped for some Indian outfits, some tops, and two very nice skirts.

On the way back Sudha informed Rene,

'Yamini didi has only one child, you know, a son. We all thought how lucky she was. You see, I couldn't have any more children after Shweta, otherwise I would have tried once more for a boy. But that was not to be. Anyway, Sanjay was a brilliant student; he went to Germany after he became a doctor, on a scholarship for his post-graduation. There he met a German girl, a Christian, and married her. That in itself was a shock for his parents, especially his father. But more was to come. He announced last year that he was becoming a Christian himself, like his wife. What this world is coming to, I don't know. You would think she would follow her husband's religion, isn't it? His father will not talk to him anymore.'

'But surely that's absurd? He is still his son, isn't he? What's wrong with following his wife's beliefs? What about Yamini bua? What does she think of all this?' Rene exclaimed.

Sudha looked at Rene as if she had taken leave of her senses. Maybe she would not be such a beneficial influence on her daughters, she thought. She said,

'Oh, Yamini didi took it badly at first, but he is her son after all, and an only child. A mother's heart forgives more easily. She keeps in touch through emails and calls him without her husband's knowledge.'

They had tea on the back porch downstairs, but Rene refused any more snacks. She brought up the subject of Nimesh again and uncle Rajan cautioned her against being very hopeful after all these years. However, it being decided by her uncle, and grudgingly agreed to by her aunt, it was soon settled that Rajan would set the wheels in motion for the search for Nimesh to begin.

Rene's two cousins, Naina and Shweta when they came, took to Rene immediately. The resemblance between Shweta and herself was striking! The older girl was a little reserved at the beginning but soon, Rene's friendliness and considerable charm had Naina warming to her. It surprised Rene to see how comfortable she felt with both sisters. All of a sudden, from having no relatives, here she was chatting away to two such adorable cousins! As uncle Rajan had predicted, the two girls loved their presents, and it was with genuine regret that they said their farewells to Rene when she left for Dadi's house after dinner.

Promises were demanded and made to meet often during her stay and plans made for a picnic at Lodhi Gardens for the following week. Uncle Rajan laughed to see the speed with which the girls had taken to one another and the thought came to him that here was proof that blood was indeed thicker than water.

Sudha, to her credit, seemed happy, because her daughters liked Rene, and that to her was a positive in Rene's favour. Yamini took a promise from Rene to visit her the week after and left with her in the car, to be dropped off two streets away. In the car, she placed a gentle hand on Rene's cheek and blurted,

'I know you think that your father, my younger brother, was a weak man, and he *was*, regarding our mother. But he wasn't heartless or bad. He did not go a happy man or without guilt, you know. Perhaps that is why he left all those things pointing towards Nimesh's existence for you to find. To somehow make amends for the way he had failed your mother.' Her eyes implored Rene for her understanding.

****

CHAPTER 16

A Date

'Get ready in your best finery. I'll show you how the rich and famous live in India. Dadi, I would have taken you, but for your knee. Therefore, I'll have to make do with Rene instead.'

This was Jai, as cool as you please, with no explanation for why he had not called her for the past two days. Rene had opened the door to the bell, the maid Swati having gone to grind some lentils required to make *dosas*, which Dadi had discovered was another Indian delicacy that Rene loved. One hand rested negligently on the door frame while he ogled shamelessly at her.

'Go on with you, you *paji* child!' giggled Dadi, charmed nonetheless.

'I am sorry, but why would I want to do that?' was Rene's dry response.

'Nice girls don't sulk, that's why. I was away in Hong Kong on a sudden business trip and two in the morning wasn't a good time to call. And I was truly flat out there. Isn't that how you Aussies say it? I am flat out, mate!'

Rene had to grin at his droll manner and idiotic accent.

'There, that's my girl! Hasn't anyone ever told you that being grumpy does *not* suit you? Yes Dadi, I would love to have your lovely chai while Rene puts on her prettiest clothes. Please be a good girl and hurry.'

Rene went up to her room to change and decided that she would give Mr. Smug down there something to ogle at. She took from the cupboard a saree which her mother had left behind on one of her visits to Nani's house. Nani had given it to her, saying,

'I would like you to have it, Dimpy. It was one of her favourites.' When Rene had protested, Nani had assured her she had another which her mother had left behind as well.

****

It was a beautiful grey-green chiffon saree with a delicate silver border throughout its length, while here and there antique silver motifs in the shape of paisleys glistened throughout the cloth.

She had a sleeveless metallic silver tank top which she wore as a blouse and wore the saree deftly over a light grey under skirt gifted also by Nani.

A pair of long silver earrings that she had bought in Kasauli completed the outfit. She left her neck bare; the silver border took care of that. A quick smoothing on of a dusky pink lipstick was all the make-up she wore. Rene slipped her feet into silver sandals and went downstairs. On the landing she paused to look at herself in a long oval mirror and felt a wave of nostalgia root her to the spot. She was wearing her mother's saree! It had touched her body. Rene lifted the free end of the saree and sniffed at it, as if her mother's smell might still linger on in its folds. She blinked away the sudden tears and resolutely made the rest of the way downstairs.

Jai's back was towards the stairs as she went down and it was Dadi's exclamation of surprise and pleasure that turned him around to stand there, staring. He had to swallow a little at the way his heart suddenly pulsed out of control.

Although her heart was beating just as fast, Rene decided it was safest to be cheeky and said airily to Jai, 'If your jaw drops any further, it will fall off entirely. Shall we go?'

To Dadi, who exclaimed how pretty she looked in a saree, she said,

'Thank you Dadi, this is my mother's saree. Nani had it with her all these years, can you believe? Oh, and I have the keys which you had given me, so please don't you or Swati trouble to wait up for me. It could get very late before we return and I can let myself in.'

When she was settled comfortably in Jai's car, she noticed he had not brought his driver. Jai turned to her and said,

'God, Rene, you look so beautiful. In that saree, you are something else! How about we ditch the wedding? Let's just disappear somewhere, you and me, hmm?'

'A wedding? To whose wedding are you planning to take me?' She decided to ignore the rest of it.

'It is a friend's sister's wedding. We've been buddies since we were at Sanawar together. I know what you are thinking. They have not invited you, etcetera. But my friend Sudesh knows about you, as in you are visiting, are my guest, well sort of. But mainly I thought, as I mentioned earlier, you might like to take in some of the social life here. Especially the stinking rich, who have more money than sense. It will be a lovely circus, I promise. Sudesh, though, is a solid guy. And you might like to see Shahrukh Khan up close and personal.

'Are you kidding me? Shahrukh Khan? Really? He's going to be there? Lead on Macduff. Oh my God, just try to stop me, mate. I am *so* going.'

'Yeah, I thought so,' was Jai's disgusted response. And rolled his eyes at her 'Aussieisms' as he privately called some of her phrases and words.

They drove quite a long way southward to the outskirts of Delhi. On the way, they passed a huge idol of Shiva, which Jai pointed out to her, and she could see the tall tower of the Qutab Minar in the distance.

****

The wedding was in a farmhouse in Chhatarpur, an erstwhile village on Delhi's southern border. It was now well known because of the many farmhouses owned by the rich and famous. It was a place to party, to hide from the media, to unwind – for celebrities, business owners, as well as wannabes with money.

The show, because that was the only way to describe the wedding, was truly all that Jai had promised. He pointed out some ministers, models, well-known journalists, a debutant actress; the party teemed with owners of business houses and celebrities. The highlight of the evening for Rene was watching the famous actor Shahrukh Khan perform from right in front of the stage. He was friendly when Sudesh introduced her, and that made her evening. After he had left, Rene felt that the atmosphere was cloying in the extreme and felt the need to get away. She turned to see Jai watching her with amusement.

'I can see how enthusiastic you are about this circus. Not my thing either. Most of those you see here are here to network, the so called chatteratti of Delhi. Now, though, you shall have the opportunity to contrast this with where I normally hang out with friends. Let's go,' he announced airily.

They left without saying goodbye, knowing that nobody was going to notice, anyway. On the way, Jai made a few calls, saying they were on their way and would reach 'there' in about half an hour.

'Where are we going?' asked Rene. She received only an enigmatic smile in response. Eventually Jai drove through the very wide, tree lined roads of a suburb called Golf Links. It was so called because of the golf course that formed the greater part of its landscape. It was very different to the rest of Delhi, with its mature trees, its aura of spaciousness, and, in all, a very tranquil look about the surroundings.

All of a sudden, they stopped before a beautiful home. It was a double storeyed white bungalow, with a charcoal tiled roof. It was large as houses went, with a narrow, curved porch and balcony jutting out gently from the centre, separating the house into two wings. Rounded Grecian columns supported the porch and balcony on the sides, softening the look.

'Whose house have we come to?' asked Rene as they stepped out of the car and as she did so, she glanced at the nameplate at the side of the gate. It said 'Miglanis' in simple brass lettering in italics, and Rene realised they had come to Jai's house. The guard, who was sitting inside a blue grey wooden lean to, sprang to his feet and opened the gates. Thankfully, he did not do any saluting but stared goggle eyed at Rene.

After greeting him, Jai gave him the car keys, and they walked through a long, wide, covered driveway to one side of the house. There was a side entrance there, and it was through that entrance that Jai and Rene entered the house.

Through a narrow but well-lit corridor, they entered the living room, which was a picture of understated elegance, yet warm and welcoming. The colours were mostly browns and rusts with deep greens and mustards to break the seriousness. A huge framed collage in black and red, which could be Goddess Durga or Kali, graced one wall. It was stunning and gave the room its colour and a certain personality. There was also an incongruous looking and much used black and mustard leather bean bag, into which Jai collapsed after seeing that Rene was seated. Here and there artefacts and mementoes were tucked in tastefully without giving the room a museum like look.

'Are you comfortable? This is my family home, by the way. Papa was smart enough to buy a house here in the days when it was still affordable. Now the prices here are really indecent and I am lucky to have somewhere to live that I don't have to pay rent for. What will you have to drink? Before my friends land up, you might as well put your legs up for a while.'

****

CHAPTER 17

New Experiences

Barely had the words left him that the doorbell stated ringing and three people, two men and a woman trooped in. Jai introduced the tall, dark man as Shanky for Shankaran and the couple as Nidhi and DK.

Nidhi smiled and chatted with Rene and winked approvingly at Jai. Behind her back and towards Jai she made a thumb's up sign. Jai just grinned at her and got busy with organising the drinks. He found some chips and dips and some salami from the fridge and soon Rene felt as if she had known all of them for a long time.

'Where the devil is Mansoor?' asked Jai after half an hour had gone by.

'You know he follows the Indian standard time. Give him an hour at least,' answered Nidhi.

'The devil is here Madame' floated a voice from the door and in entered a delicate featured, handsome man of medium height. He walked into the room, first hugging Nidhi as he did so, and then Jai and Shanky. His eyes gleamed appreciatively at Rene upon being introduced.

Rene joined in the conversation when she could and they all made sure that she did. But mostly she just observed Jai. How relaxed he was with his friends, how intelligently they all spoke about everything. But there was something that set Jai apart from the rest. He was good-looking, but then, so was Mansoor. They were all pleasant, successful people, but there was a certain confidence in Jai, a certain softness in his look. Jai turned in that moment and caught her look. An answering awareness came over him and he wished with all his being that everyone would go home and leave them alone.

DK nudged Nidhi and raised his eyebrows at Jai. Jai put on his bland face and took out the food that he had ordered from the nearby Khan Market, and headed towards the enormous kitchen to heat it in the microwave. He had two people living in the servant's quarters behind the main house, but he refused to wake them up at this late hour. Nidhi and Rene elected to help and soon they were sitting with their plates full of *kathi* kebabs, tandoori chicken, *roomali roti*, daal, mint chutney and salad.

The smell was appetising and Rene, who had a healthy appetite, soon tucked in, forgetting her fears of a Delhi belly. She loved the taste of the roomali roti, a very thin large chapatti, so called because it was as thin as a *roomal*, a handkerchief.

DK and Mansoor favoured rum and were unimaginatively nicknamed old and young monk, respectively. The rest had either whiskey or vodka. Rene herself nursed her one glass of Malibu and pineapple juice cocktail through the entire evening, or what was left of it. It was three in the morning by the time the last of Jai's friends had left. Jai asked Rene to stay the night when he saw that she was dropping on her feet.

'I'll drive myself to work and get my driver to drop you off later. My Dad's car happens to be parked here while they are holidaying in Europe. Just sleep in. I'll be as quiet as I can. You can borrow one of my mom's nightdresses or I could lend you a shirt, if you like,' he offered.

'Don't they live here too?' asked Rene, surprised. She thought Jai hesitated an infinitesimal second before he spoke.

'After Dad retired, they settled in Dehradun. The pollution in Delhi was bad for Mum's asthma. She hasn't had a single attack since they've settled there. They drive down once in a while or I go up to see them.'

Jai took her arm as they went up the stairs. "The bedrooms are all upstairs, except the one on the ground floor which I had converted from a study, to accommodate dad's painful knee,' he said.

The bedroom she was to sleep in was beautifully, but simply furnished. Jai bent to kiss her on the cheek, but the tension that had been building in both of them suddenly sought release. His arms encircled her waist while her own stole around his neck. There was an urgency in the meeting of their lips, a hunger which there was only one way to satisfy.

It seemed so totally natural when Jai scooped Rene up in his arms and walked straight on down the corridor to his own room. A double bed with a white, quilted bedspread was all she had a glimpse of before Jai laid her down gently on it. Afterwards, Rene had little recollection of whether Jai undressed her or whether she did so herself. All she knew was that she wanted Jai to hold her, kiss her, and that she was on fire. She wanted more than the paltry kisses that they had so far shared. She gave herself to him with an abandon that would have frightened her if she had stopped to think about it. But thinking was something she did not want to do just yet.

It was apparent that neither did Jai want to bother with thinking at the moment. He was as passionate as he was gentle. Jai was very much in danger of feeling for Rene, much more than just passion. His feelings were apparent in every look, every touch. Although he did not quite know it, he was in love, and it showed in the way he made love to Rene.

A small cry made him pause, but Rene persuaded him to go on, her eyes speaking for her. He hugged her later and kissed her again and again, as if sorry that he was the first.

He put his arms about her, and Rene went to sleep like that.

Sometime in the early hours of the morning, she stirred and realised that Jai's arms were still wrapped around her and that he was staring seriously down at her.

'An Aussie virgin. I am surprised at you!' Jai remarked in an attempt to lighten the mood.

'What's so surprising? We don't all jump into bed with the first available guy, you know.' Rene paused, realising that he was teasing. She said in a more matter-of-fact way, 'Sure, I had a boyfriend or two and we kissed and stuff, but I never felt like going all the way with any of them. Just didn't happen.'

The last was said with a cushion pushed on top of Jai's face.

'What was that for?' Jai asked, laughing.

'To wipe that smirk off your face,' was her rejoinder.

His eyes were alight with amusement. As he looked at her, his expression changed and he pulled her to him, saying,

'I am not laughing at you. I was just surprised, that's all. I mean not because you're from Australia or anything. I mean, in this day and age. I don't know what the hell I do mean, but are you sure about this?'

Rene just flung her arms around his neck, kissed him, saying, 'Guys just talk. What does a girl do to get some action?'

Jai did a low growl and, trying to sound wicked, said, 'Ah, so the lady wants action. Hmm, I can't disappoint her now, can I? Let's see now....' And he did not disappoint. Afterwards, lying in Jai's arms, Rene said,

'It's so weird that my first time has been in India. It may come as a surprise to you, especially after seeing the young people here, but a lot of us are pretty sheltered out there. Till year twelve and my high school exams, my world was home, school, ballet, netball and band. Suddenly at eighteen I could go to pubs, drink alcohol and party. My friends and I would hang out at pubs, have a drink or two, but I never really enjoyed pub crawling. Our thing was movies, dancing and partying. Also swimming and shopping. And I hadn't met a guy who could make me feel like this.'

Rene attempted to make light of her suddenly fierce feelings. Funny, she sounded as if she was apologising for being a virgin!

'I'll share my secret passion. My very special obsession – trying every flavour, old and new at every ice cream place there is in Sydney. Once I have tried a few dozen still left, I'll get into Guinness,' she laughed.

As Jai played with a few of her curls, she turned on her stomach to look at him and added,

'Dad had this curfew time of twelve in the night. If I wasn't home by then, he would call continuously till I was back. So, I made sure I was back by then. Most of my friends had parents like that and to tell you the truth, while it was awfully annoying then, now I am glad that I had a dad who cared what became of me and watched over me. I actually got quite a culture shock at the way the kids were letting their hair down at the wedding today, with no inhibitions in front of their parents! While many of us are not virgins, we wouldn't be feeling each other up like that in front of ours, I can tell you that! Did you notice the girl in a purple dress with the tall, thin guy? They were all but making out right there, in the middle of the dance floor!'

'Yes, I did, more because of the open mouthed way you were gawking. They were probably stoned, like many at the party. The smell of pot in the air around was quite strong, you know.'

'And you would know what it was, how?' Rene asked with a smirk.

'Yeah, okay, some of the guys at school smoked it and having tried it once and fainted, much to my subsequent mortification, I didn't much care to try it again. The only other thing I had tried when I was a teenager was *bhaang*, cannabis, you know. But that's a story for another day,' answered Jai.

'Oh no, you don't. I want to hear it now, get to know your debauched past and all.' Rene wasn't about to let him off so easily. She also wanted to know everything there was to know about him.

'Wait till you hear the whole tragic story. It was the morning of the Holi festival. We had this large shrub growing in our garden and we didn't know what it was until that morning when we saw our gardener Buddhi collecting the leaves in a large basket. I was fifteen and Sandy thirteen. We were waiting for our friends to come to play with the Holi colours. Having nothing better to do to occupy ourselves with while doing so, we went to Buddhi and asked him what he was going to do with the leaves.

"Oh, these are bhaang leaves. I am going to make *thandaai* for the Holi guests," Buddhi said.

'*Thandaai*? What's that?' I asked him.

"It's a traditional drink for Holi. You don't know? But then, how would you? You're too young to have had it, of course. It's quite tasty, though," declared Buddhi.

The moment he said that, I decided I was going to have it, too young be damned.

'How do you make it?' I persisted.

"Oh, I just grind the leaves, add milk and sugar. Some of it my wife will mix with *besan* to make pakoras for a snack. But you boys are making me late and *saabji* will be angry if I don't have them ready before the guests come," Buddhi said distractedly and shuffled off in the direction of the back entrance of the house.

The minute we saw the door close, Sandy and I ran to the shrub, stuffing our pockets full of the leaves. Sandy sneaked out the mini blender from the kitchen and I suddenly had a thirst for a cup of milk. In my room we blended the leaves with a little milk which already had sugar in it. Well, at the time we hadn't realised that the proportion of the paste to milk was about a few tablespoons to a jug and here we were with a cup worth of dark green cannabis paste with barely two tablespoons of milk.

Well, we drank almost half a cup of the filthy tasting drink each, neither Sandy nor me admitting to wanting to give up. Anyway, what happened next is told and retold at every family or friends' gathering where Sana is present, much to our embarrassment.'

'Oh my God, I am beginning to suspect it was one of those life changing experiences. Who's Sana?' Rene exclaimed. She looked out of the window and saw that the sky had already lightened and she lost the desire to sleep.

'I haven't told you about my sister Sana, have I? Don't ever mention that to her, will you? She'd have my hide. Sana is the youngest of the Miglanis, four years younger than Sandy. She's in the US at the moment, finishing her research in particle physics. You would like her, bossy woman though she is. And Sana was the only one who didn't get to partake of the infamous bhaang, although she begged to have the pretty green drink, please,' laughed Jai.

'So, what happened? You guys got drunk?' asked Rene, intensely curious by now.

'Drunk? We were stoned, high as kites, but not like any kind of stoned that you can imagine. We didn't know then that bhaang plays with your brain. I was making all kinds of faces, stretching my jaws till they ached for two days afterwards. Then, I decided that our first-floor balcony was a helipad, and that I was a helicopter. I 'flew' out but fortunately got only a few bloody scratches from the casuarina tree which caught me as I fell through it.'

By now Rene was laughing hysterically at the picture that created.

'However, the highlight of the day was Sandy's performance. He was studying Macbeth at school and he got it into his head that he was Lady Macbeth and kept incessantly repeating 'out damned spot' and washing his hands constantly. When mom saw him enter the bathroom for the fifth time, she asked Sandy what he thought he was doing, to which he replied morosely,

"Can't you see the bloodstains? They will just not wash off!"

Mom realised then that something was seriously wrong, and that we were not just playing the fool. At that moment, I came in from outside with some of my scratches bleeding.

The lowlight of the episode was that three slaps were administered that evening. Dad slapped and cuffed Sandy on the ear, but he was so out of it he can't remember.

The awe inspiring slap of the day was handed out by Buddhi's wife right across her husband's face. Buddhi had found the leftover paste in our glass and swallowed it all, followed by a generously heaped plate of the bhaang fritters. His intoxication level was so high that he could not find his mouth to smoke his *beedi* cigarette. He had put it down on the table but somehow when he lifted it, the lighted end was towards him; Buddhi was in the act of putting that end into his mouth when his wife came into the room. He singed his moustache before she pulled it from his hand and then delivered the slap. Fortunately for her, he doesn't remember it either. Looking scared, she promptly went to the shelf where she kept all her idols, beating her chest a few times, asking forgiveness for slapping her *pati dev* – 'in house God', you know!' Jai said, chuckling at the memory.

'You said that there were three slaps. Who slapped *you*?' Rene asked.

'Very clever! Mom slapped me. But more than the slap, it was the look in her eyes and words when she said,

"You have disappointed me more than I could have ever imagined, Jai. I never expected this of you."

Much later, she owned that Sandy and I had been more sinned against than sinning, that we really hadn't known what we were doing or how dangerous bhaang really was. But that day, seeing the tears in her eyes made me feel really small and, when I went to her room to apologise, she made me swear I would never touch any drugs or alcohol ever, and I readily did so.

Years later, she relented on the alcohol, though. And although she didn't like me smoking cigarettes, she didn't say much about it.'

'Haven't seen you smoking though,' interposed Rene.

'It was a phase. Maybe two or three a day? I just needed a push to stop, and that's another strange story. It happened while I was travelling on the train to Mumbai. A young woman with a little boy, around eight or nine years old, was travelling in the same compartment. After a while, when I went out of the carriage to where I could have a smoke, the little boy came out to go to the toilet. When he came out, I had lit my cigarette, and the boy came near, staring up at me. When I looked at him, he said,

"Hello there! You'll die of cancer, you know that? And serve you right, too!"

It took me a few seconds to recover and though I thought he was just being a smartass, I said nothing to him.

At that moment, the boy's mother had come looking for him, wondering what was taking her son so long. She heard the last part of her son's speech and hastily apologised to me.

"I am *so* sorry! He has been approaching total strangers whom he sees smoking. It's because," As she spoke, she became teary and the boy wrapped his arms around her, sobbing. When he quietened, the mother said that she had lost her husband some weeks ago to lung cancer and that she was going to her parents' home with her son for some time.

Impulsively, I put out the cigarette and gave it to the boy, asking him to chuck it out of the open door, while I held on to his other arm. I thought at the time that it would make him quiet, get him off my back. After that, it was the end of smoking for me. Pretty corny, don't you think?

And so, now you have it, except for the teetotaller bit, you have before you the perfect candidate for the Indian matrimonial column – 'tall, fair, handsome, x figure salary, does not do drugs, does not smoke, just what moms ordered for their equally perfect daughters,' Jai grinned.

'Hmm, yes. Only you forgot to add exceptionally modest, you narcissist!'

In answer, Jai drew her to him and kissed her. Having decided that there was not much point in trying to sleep, Rene made her way to the bathroom. Today was the day uncle Rajan would call her to let her know of any progress in their search for the whereabouts of Nimesh, and she wanted to be there to receive his call.

****

CHAPTER 18

A Lead at Last

The call, when it came, was not promising at all. Uncle Rajan had drawn a complete blank in his search so far. He had sent a few of his constables to each of the seven well known *dheras* where most of the hijras of Delhi lived. They had very little to go on with. A name with no last name. That was to appease Sudha, so that no one could trace any connection back to her family. Not that a last name would be likely to be of any help. Most young boys who had left their homes or had been turned out from theirs did not use their last names any more. It was also so long ago. Even their names would have changed to female names. Rene had at least a clue that her brother's name may be Nimesha now, from the mementoes in the suitcase.

Apparently, according to uncle Rajan's sources, the hijras lived in ghettoes, in houses known as dheras. Each such group or household lived like a family within the hijra community, he had informed her. The guru of every household was the head of the family, treated like a mother. There could also be a *dadaguru* or the grandmother and the *purdahguru* or the great grandmother. The rest were disciples known as *chelas* and together they formed a family. Sometimes a guru who was growing old would select one chela to be a successor and she would then train the chela for her new role.

Over the years, the gurus and members of the houses would probably have changed several times, making it even more difficult to locate Nimesh.

A week went by with no luck in finding any trace of where Nimesh could be found. Then, on Friday, just as Rene was sitting at her laptop, bringing Seema and Helen up to date with what was going on in her search so far, a tiny, but sure ray of hope brought Rene out of her current pessimistic frame of mind.

Shahala, a hijra, who had once earned her living by prostitution, but now too old to do so, heard of the enquiries the police were making. She took special interest because the head constable asking questions was one whom she knew, the only one who had been kind to her and had more or less saved her life.

As a young boy, Shahala's parents had turned her out of her home when they had discovered that their son, then called Karim, liked doing the chores that his sisters were asked to do and enjoyed playing with dolls. Karim had preferred to spend hours on intricate embroidery instead of doing what other boys did. He began cross dressing and tried to make friends with the girls in his school and neighbourhood. Soon, however, he found that the boys avoided him, making fun of his effeminacy, and parents banned the girls from playing with him. In the society that he lived in, girls and boys did not play together.

One day, he saw some hijras begging at a traffic light. After many days of watching their routine, he drew some courage and waited for them to come toward the decrepit looking dhaba where they normally ate their home made lunch or drank tea. He approached their table and sobbed out his story, begging them to take him with them. Upon hearing his story, at first the hijras advised him to wait till he had finished his schooling, but Karim was adamant.

After a month, Karim ran away to become Shahala, with the hijra she had befriended in the group. Shahala was attractive, with her large doe eyes and her hair curling down to her waist. It was easy to mistake her for a woman because of her delicate features. Her guru taught her how to wear make-up and she had her ears pierced. At first, she received training in singing and dancing. Shahala tried to make a living out of the hijra's chief occupation, which involved performing *badhai* at weddings, at the birth of a child, or even when a someone built a new house. She enjoyed singing and dancing in order to bless the newly married couples and newborn babies.

Sadly, though, the earnings from performing at these events were not enough to buy basic necessities, let alone saving up for her castration procedure. Sumati, one of the senior members of her gharana, tried to dissuade her from going through with the procedure if she did not want to. But Shahala wanted the transformation to her female self to be complete, with no option of turning back.

She started adding to her income by begging at traffic lights, as she had seen other hijras do. When that was not enough either, she started dancing in bars. Her looks drew men to her and eventually, driven by poverty, she took the plunge into prostitution. She had been raped twice; once by a policeman and once by a pimp who wanted to teach her a lesson for encroaching on the turf reserved for 'normal' sex workers.

It was during a similar situation, when two policemen were holding her while another was about to assault her, that Avadesh, who had been a junior constable in those days, had come upon them. Picking up a rock from the roadside, he hit one of them and threatened to report them to their wives, scaring them away. He knew that threatening to report them to the police would cut no ice. He had then helped clean Shahala's wounds and escorted her to her dhera.

Shahala had never forgotten the only person outside her community who had treated her like a human being, amongst a sea of inhuman parasites. When she heard him making enquiries about Nimesh, she waited till he was walking back towards his jeep, and under pretence of soliciting him, told him,

'Go to Sumati. She will know where Nimesha is. Tell her I sent you. Speak to no one else. She is very old now and lives in that yellow and blue dhera, the one with the brown door. Now go!'

She let out a peal of laughter and, with a suggestive sway of her hips towards Avadesh, she turned towards her house.

As soon as uncle Rajan called to give her this news, Rene quickly shut down her laptop and, seeing that it was still only four in the afternoon, prepared to leave immediately. Feeling instinctively that whoever this Sumati was, she was more likely to talk to her than a policeman, Rene asked her uncle whether she could go straight away.

Uncle Rajan found out from their police communication radio that Avadesh was not very far from Maharani Bagh at that moment and agreed that Rene could go provided that Avadesh accompanied her.

****

CHAPTER 19

Sumati

Sumati lived in one of the larger ghettoes in the Seelampur area. Something about the place felt familiar to Rene. There were plastic bags of all hues and piles of garbage on either side of what purported to call itself a lane, leading to a motley collection of houses, which were nothing but slum dwellings for the most part. As Rene made her way from the car with Avadesh, gingerly picking her way through the garbage, trying not to step on cow dung and litter, she was suddenly brought up short by four hijras who stood there, barring her way.

'Turn around, measure your footsteps and march back the way you came,' said the tallest of them all. She was ugly; the white patchy make-up on her face caked and streaked while her eyes glowered with hate at Avadesh. A black mole pulsed angrily on her right cheek. Her eyes swivelled towards Rene, and the expression in them did not change.

'I have come to meet Sumati. She knows I am coming. Please let us pass,' Rene said.

'Oye *memsaab*! We know why you have come and we don't want you here. Take your pretty face and go back to wherever you came from. Unless.... you have a taste for the likes of us?' she leered.

'Now see here,' began Avadesh, 'you let Sumati decide who she will meet. Move.'

The other hijras looked at the tall one, but she did not move. They did not budge, either.

Shahala was sitting on the step of her one-room shack with some kind of greenish paste, possibly henna, smeared all over her hair. She was drawing a pattern with some left-over paste on the palm of her hand.

'Looks like some people are born to spend their lives in jail. This man is the police, you fool! The one who helped me, remember? But carry on. You are doing a great job. Once was not enough for you, it appears,' she drawled, without looking up from her drawing.

At the word jail, the tall one had frozen in terror, her face like curdled milk. Once, not so very long ago, she had been dragged by the hair, screaming, from the street where she was soliciting customers. Two policemen had taken her to a jail, raped and beaten her to within an inch of her life and thrown her back on the street, bleeding and left for dead. All the bluster was driven out of her, and she turned and left without another glance or word. As she passed in front of Shahala though, she spat on the ground in front of her.

Shahala pointed to a yellowing, semi-finished house, some of the bricks still left unrendered. One grey window shutter dangled on broken hinges.

'Sumatiguru's house. Don't take *him* in there,' she said, pointing to Avadesh.

A chela ushered them into the house. Rene asked Avadesh to wait outside. Sumati must have heard and called out for him to come in as well. The room that Rene entered was decorated in bright colours. Multi coloured cushions which had seen better days rested against the wall on a divan bed. It looked reasonably clean. Garish nylon flowers adorned a few plastic vases. The walls were a bright pink. Every table was covered with hand crocheted and incongruously pretty lace covers. There was a hand quilted rug on the bed and a rough woollen one on the floor. The smell of strong jasmine from incense sticks filled the room.

Sumati sat in one of the two chairs in the room. She was a rather tall woman, slim and dark. A ring twinkled on her nose and she had tied her hair in a bun. A *gajra* made of Mogra jasmine flowers ringed her bun. She was not heavily made up like some of her chelas, with just a light touch of kohl lining her eyes. Her neck and ears were adorned with costume jewellery. She looked like she may have been attractive in her youth, but age and a hard life had taken its toll and lines ran under her eyes and down the sides of her nose and lips.

She saw Rene looking at the lone framed photograph of a man, adorned with a garland of flowers made of sandalwood. She smiled a little sadly and informed Rene that it was a photograph of her now dead husband.

Sumati peered short sightedly at Rene, arched her brows and smiling with her lips stretched to one side, said,

'So. You have come to look for Nimesha after all these years! Well, you might as well know right now that this is the reason she went from here in the first place. Your mother had tried and almost succeeded in finding her, too. She had discovered this place through her contacts and we had seen her sitting outside in her car, hoping to find her son. You must be the little sister he used to talk about all the time. He never spoke about his mother, but I used to hear him cry at night with her picture under his pillow.'

Rene shivered at the picture that was created in her mind by Sumati's words but only said,

'Do you know where he, I mean she, is now?'

'I know where I sent her, but I cannot say where she could be now. I did not want to. Send her, I mean. She was such an obedient, helpful child. I never needed to scold her for anything. She learnt everything very easily and would have been such an asset to our family. She would read to me and even used to massage my tired legs sometimes,' Sumati sighed.

'But why did you send her then?' Rene asked.

'I did it for her. She saw her mother one day and would not go out of the dhera after that. She kept pleading with me to send her to some other place, anywhere, as long as it was far away from Dilli,' continued Sumati. Rene realized now why the surroundings were familiar. She must have waited outside just these slums with her mother in the blue car.

'I was very worried when I sent her on the train to Benaras,' Sumati continued. 'All our chelas are like family. People wonder about us. How we behave, do we care about anyone, do we kidnap children? There are bad people everywhere. Our community is no exception. But we care for our family. The guru is like a mother, you know. I bitterly regret sending her all alone. That is why I agreed to talk to you, to help you today. It has weighed heavily on my mind all these years. If you ever find her, will you please let me know?' Sumati almost pleaded.

'But how will I find her in Benaras?' Rene was anxious now.

'I will give you a letter for Rashmi, to whom I sent Nimesha. She lives not very far from the ghats in…., let me see, Shivdaspur, yes. I have not seen her for a long time but I believe that old crow is still alive. I hope you find her there. Maybe you will be successful where your mother wasn't.'

'Oye!' Sumati called out to one of her chelas. 'Get some tea and samosas for the lady. She is the sister of one of our own. Hurry up, don't dawdle! Very lazy, this one!'

While she dictated the letter to one of her chelas who could read and write, Avadesh stood up to fetch the car as close to the house as he could. As Rene touched the delicately woven lace of the table next to her, Sumati smiled sadly and said,

'These laces and the quilt were made by Bina, one of my sweetest chelas. She was very talented, came from a rich home. But after being abandoned by her family and ostracised by society, she was as destitute as the rest of us. Who cares whether we have any talent, whether we are intelligent, how we earn our livelihood? Most of us don't know where our next meal will come from. They murdered poor Bina in Kalindi, near the river. Two of my other chelas have died recently of AIDS. I sincerely hope that you will find your sister in good health. May Bahuchara Mata be with you.'

Sumati handed the letter to Rene, and Avadesh brought the car. Rene stood, and thanking Sumati for her help, she put an envelope with some money quietly on the lace cover of the table near the door and left.

****

CHAPTER 20

Naina

Jai came to see her the day after, to say that he was going to Singapore on a business trip and would be away for three or four days. He took one look at her and exclaimed,

'Why, you look all in! Rene, you mustn't go on like this without a break, sweetheart. You will make yourself ill with all the running around that you have been doing for the last few days. Promise me you will take the time to unwind with your cousins till I come back. Better still, come with me to Singapore. It's only for three days. I'm going there just to tie up some loose ends on a new proposal.' He kissed her quickly, seeing that she was alone.

'And what am I supposed to do there while you hobnob with the big business bosses? I have been to Singapore a couple of times and apart from the amazing food, it's a pretty boring place, I have to say. And so humid! I promise I will take a break and spend time with my cousins till you get back.' Rene looked around quickly to see if anyone was watching and teased,

'And do you think you could maybe kiss me with a little more courage than this tentative sample, hmm?' Not needing further encouragement or challenge, Jai drew her into his arms to do just that.

****

True to her word, Rene spent the next two days with her cousins. It was a unique experience for Rene to find how much the two girls liked her and how they already treated her as one of them, as another sister. They went picnicking and sightseeing at the Qutab Minar and the lovely ruins of the Purana Kila and then went shopping at the quaint but lovely Hauz Khas Village and Mehrauli markets. Her eyes shot up into her forehead at the prices but she found a lovely jacket that suited her pocket.

The next day, Naina and Shweta took her to the home of one of Naina's friends, where a party was in full swing. Shweta was especially thrilled, as she was not normally allowed to go to Naina's parties. Rene and the girls were having a good time chatting and dancing until a tall, bearded young man walked in with an attractive looking girl in a red dress hanging on his arm. He saw Naina and stopped in the middle of greeting his hostess. The girl on his arm turned to see what he was staring at and her face flushed with anger when she saw Naina.

Naina, meanwhile, was digging her fingers rather hard into Rene's wrist. She whispered,

'Let's go, I don't want a scene.' She stood up, but it was already too late. The young man walked towards her and said,

'Hi Naina. I didn't know you were coming too.'

'Nor did I,' Naina replied.

'Yeah,' he smiled. 'You wouldn't have come then, would you?'

'Perhaps.' Naina smiled wryly. 'Rohit, how about you just let it go? By the way, your new girlfriend is sending looks that could sear me on the spot. I need to take my cousin home, if you don't mind.'

'Oh hello, I didn't realise. Nice to meet you. Hi Shwets, didn't see you either. Naina, there is something I need to talk to you about. Could you meet me, say tomorrow evening? I really need to talk to you.'

'Why, what would we say to each other? Oh, oh.' This was because the girl in the red dress had reached them and, with her lips curled in distaste, said,

'You really are desperate or what? Why can't you leave him alone? Why are you always following him around, Naina? He's so over you, you know.'

To her credit, Naina just raised her eyebrows and smiled disbelievingly and with a wave towards her hostess, walked out with Rene and Shweta in tow.

'What was all that about? Of course, you can tell me to mind my business.' exclaimed Rene in awe, having witnessed the very first *scene* of her life.

At first, she got no reply from Naina, who was driving quite fast for her usually sedate speed, as if to put as much distance as she could from her friend's house.

'As you may have guessed, Rohit is, well, was my friend. Actually, he was more than that. We were engaged till about a month ago.' explained Naina. Rene waited. She glanced at Shweta. Naina caught the look and continued,

'Don't worry, she knows everything. Mummy always sent her with us everywhere we went, as a chaperone. We have known each other since we were in high school and we were neighbours too. His family is from the same state, same everything, if you know what I mean. So, even though it was a 'love match', mummy and papa were okay with it.

But soon, the cracks began to appear. Not between Rohit and me, but between his sister and I, and with his mother, who did not like me much either.'

'So? What went wrong? You weren't marrying *them*!' Rene interjected.

'It is different here. A marriage in India is a marriage of families, not just the couple. It is not so much that something went wrong. They discovered that I was very different from them. I am not their kitty party type. I wanted to continue to work after we married. They didn't want me to. There was no need, they told me, rich as they were. They spent their days in kitties, parlours and shopping. Sheila, his sister, was quite a mean type, actually. I saw her slap her maid because she had dropped and broken one of their special crystal glasses. Bit scary!

I was working with an NGO at the time. Rohit's family did not want me involved in the so called dangerous social work 'activities' as they called them. They are extremely superficial people. They would be happy for me to wear diamonds and expensive clothes and sit around looking pretty. We just didn't understand each other.

I tried really hard to be nice to them, tried to involve them in what I do. To make them understand why I do what I do. But it was a no go. It's kind of funny, really. I think they would have preferred me to be an empty head, even slightly bad. They believed my trying to be nice to them was some kind of act. That I was a bit of a pretend goody two shoes. I felt they wanted me to be doing something stupid, even wrong. It would have been easier to for them to accept that I am fallible and be in a position to forgive me, you know. It was harder for them to believe that I could truly try to do something from the goodness of my heart, that I could possibly be a genuinely good person. I didn't fit the mould. The mould was in an unchangeable cast, from their point of view.

Rohit's sister said as much to me when we broke up. It's amazing how many people see those who want to do good with suspicion. They feel that somehow you are trying to be holier than thou. It makes them uncomfortable. They'd rather you be a little bad than too good. Sort of brings everyone to the same level, I suppose. It's a strange world that we live in, Rene. I must sound weirdly philosophical, but then I have had a lot of time to think about what went wrong.

As for Rohit, his best suggestion was that I take a break till we got married, wait maybe a year. In the meantime, they would get to know me better, see me as I really am and he would get them around to agreeing to let me continue my work, telling me how important it was that we start on a happy note etcetera,' Naina explained.

'But that's so hypocritical!' exclaimed Rene.

'Exactly! It would also be a kind of cheating them and me. I couldn't give up my work for a year and expect it back on a platter. It doesn't work that way, here. I want to start my own NGO, going forward. And it all seemed so ridiculously false to me I said no. I would have to live with them unless I made a stand about living separately. It would be a pattern of fighting for everything I believed in, fighting for our happiness at every turn. I broke the engagement because I saw that between his family and me, he would be torn, and I just wasn't up to tolerating their manipulations anymore.'

'Are you going to meet him, then?' asked Rene.

'Not likely. I want to put it behind me now. Even if he wants to say that we can live somewhere else or that I could work, he *is* their only son with a partnership in his dad's law firm. I don't want him to resent me for taking him away from his family, maybe even his work; *that* is important to him too. And didn't you see Ketaki, the one in the red dress? She is not likely to let him out of sight for the next few months at least, believe me!'

Shweta piped in, saying, 'You do kind of sound very unforgiving, you know. If Rohit bhaiya is willing to give this relationship one more chance, you could at least meet him halfway.'

Naina rounded on her sister. 'Is that what it seems like? That I'm not willing to give Rohit another chance out of pique? You think I am just being revengeful, I suppose. I wish I could make you, mummy, everyone, understand that it is not it at all. I have gone over that hump ages ago. It's all a bit of an anticlimax now. Unfortunately, time has...' she paused. 'I don't know how to describe it; time and I guess stress has diluted my feelings for him. And that scares me not a little. I am actually glad we didn't marry then, if my feelings have turned out to be so shallow, I mean.'

'Why don't you meet him just once and see what he has to say at least. If nothing else, you will not keep wondering and regretting that you didn't give him a chance. What if his family has changed their attitude towards you, at least your work? If not, nothing changes anyway,' suggested Rene.

'Not likely that they will change. But maybe you're right. I should meet him once, if only to get a proper closure on this relationship.' replied Naina. Her heart, though, had little hope that anything much would come of it.

****

CHAPTER 21

Not a Playboy

Jai came back in three days, as promised. He took her out for a meal to a strange little restaurant called D's Biryani in Defence Colony, or Def Col, as the locals preferred to call it. Strange, because the roof was attached to the underside of a flyover road above, which shook every time someone drove a heavy vehicle over it. Rene tried not to jump each time that happened. Jai noticed and said laughingly,

'Don't worry, it's not going to fall on our heads, at least it hasn't in the last ten years.'

They ate the most aromatic and delicious biryani that Rene had ever eaten and a kathi kabab roll each, washed down with a glass of rose lassi. Too full for dessert, Rene and Jai made their way to his car. As she made to sit, Jai said,

'Do you mind if we take a minor detour to my office? I need to drop off a file to my assistant, who is waiting for this. He is going on leave for a week starting tomorrow and wants to finish with this before he goes. That is, if you are not in too much of a hurry to get back.'

Rene was not and told Jai as much. Jai instructed Bhola, his driver, to change his route accordingly. As he opened his side of the door to get out of the car, Rene said,

'Could I come in too? If you don't mind, of course? Just curious to see the great man's office, that's all.'

Jai only smiled enigmatically and took Rene with him, past the blue grey, double doored high gates and up the lifts to the fifth floor of the office building. He rented both the fourth and the fifth floors, a few of the windows still showing light even at this hour.

Rene's eyes rounded in awe at the grandeur of his office when she saw it. It was huge as offices went and decorated very elegantly. A big walnut table topped with green baize stood to one side and beige blinds complemented the chocolate and beige patterned parquet floor. Rene made her way to a two-seater chesterfield in mahogany to the far side of the room and found that there was already a teapot with tea and biscuits waiting for them, on a small coffee table in front of the sofa.

Jai picked up the phone and, in response to his call, a stocky, bespectacled man in his early forties came in. He didn't see Rene sitting to the side and bounded in, saying,

'Hi boss. You will be glad to know that we have done away with the need for that damned middle man and….' He paused at Jai's gesture with his head towards Rene, and his face was comical in its expression of dismay.

'That's all right. Please ignore me and carry on with whatever you are doing. Just pretend I am not there,' Rene smiled.

At that moment the door opened again to admit a slim, iron haired woman.

'Why, Mrs. Batliwala, what are you doing here still?' exclaimed Jai.

'I was about to leave when I heard you were coming. I stayed because I had something I need to talk to you about after you have finished talking to Mr. Parag here.' She turned to go as she finished speaking and saw Rene as she did so. Her eyes widened, and she raised her eyebrows at Jai, a slightly disapproving turn to her lips making her seem more like a mother than a secretary.

'Oh, and Mrs. B, this is my 'cousin' Rene, you know, the one from Australia?'

Mrs. Batliwala's brow cleared, and suddenly she was all affection and graciousness.

'Yes, yes, the one who called and called till you spoke to her. Didn't you go to Kasauli with her? How are you, child? It's nice to meet you finally. But you must be so bored here, *dikra*. Would you like to see the rest of the office? I will be happy to show you around. Let these children do their work.' Mrs. Batliwala, it seemed, knew all the finer details of Jai's personal life as well as his official one, Rene thought to herself, smiling amusedly.

'Oh, would you? That would be lovely. Yes, the um children might be better off without us for now,' Rene giggled. 'Does everyone talk like this to their employers here?' she continued to Mrs. Batliwala.

'No, no dikra, everywhere it is very formal, very formal. No first names even, mostly. Sir this, madam that. Or mister, missus. But Jai Miglani is different; he does not care for these formalities. However, don't you be fooled by how we talk to him. He is deeply respected and no one here takes their work lightly. He works hard and expects everyone to do likewise. Yet he finds the time to joke, ask after everyone's family. There is hardly anyone's name, birthday or anniversary he does not remember, anyone's illness or circumstances of which he is unaware. And mind you, I have known him for over ten years; he takes care of his staff like he would his own family. He doesn't do it just to comply with employment welfare and such like, but because he genuinely cares for us all.'

Rene did not know how to respond to this. She felt not a little pride at this enigma that was Jai, a respect mingling with her liking for him. She stopped short at the thought, a very worried young woman, not at all sure where all these feelings were taking her.

Freny, as Mrs. Batliwala was christened, but not called that by anyone other than her husband until Rene insisted upon it, gave her a guided tour of both floors. She was particularly proud of the new parquet floors in the offices and the modern kitchen. The fourth floor was given to the real estate and shipping divisions while the upper floor housed the garment export division as well as the offices of the CEO, the Human Resources department, marketing and finance heads and the company lawyer. It was all very eye opening because she had no idea that he ran so many diverse businesses. By the time they returned to his office, Jai was standing at the door, Parag having left.

On their way to Dadi's house, Rene turned her head towards Jai and said,

'Your parents must be very proud of you, right? To have their son achieve all this at such a young age must be quite something for them!'

Jai was silent and Rene was so frighteningly attuned to his feelings by now that she sensed straight away that she had touched a raw nerve.

'It's all right. I am not prying,' she said quickly, glancing at him sideways.

'I wish he was. Proud of me. My dad, that is,' said Jai, taking her by surprise. 'Let's take a walk in that park, shall we? Of course, if you are not terribly tired?'

They walked into the park and sat on one of the many green benches there. Jai was silent for a space and then said, 'My dad, he is my stepdad. No, it was not all that bad, don't look like that. He wasn't really a bad person, just very weak. Most of the time, he was full of bluster and trying hard to prove that he was a powerful man. Not that he ever harmed me physically. In fact, I wouldn't have minded a slap or two if required. But the constant attempt at trying to please him from the time I was around five years old until I was nearly eighteen was wearing me down mentally. My step brother would get into all kinds of scrapes, the usual teenage stuff, whereas I would try to be all the things that my dad would like me to be. Still, I could never please him.

It wasn't as if he was cruel or mean, but to this day, I have never heard a word of appreciation from him. Not once. He would lecture both of us on doing well at school, but when I did do very well, there would never be a word from him. A nod meaning that's just what was expected, no big deal was all that I was ever going to get; but I didn't realise that until I was older. For my sake, at least, it was not too late.

Every idea that I had, every opinion, whether it was about sports, politics, career or hobbies, would be a source of argument. I would argue back, sometimes heatedly, while mum would kick me under the table or frown at me to stop. She could never say anything to him, probably because she believed that she owed him somehow. She felt she owed him that loyalty for having accepted me as his own.

After a point, I stopped retaliating. In fact, I went to the other extreme of not arguing at all. At that point in my life, a quote in a book by a famous author had impressed me greatly. It went something like, 'A person convinced against his will is of the same opinion still.' So I decided not to react to his bigoted and inane statements. Neither did I nod at those he made in self-praise. In hindsight, I feel, I think that maybe if I had actually argued with him, even had a slanging match, he would have known how to deal with it. He would have argued till forever and shouted me down as usual, ending with how I could never come first in class; or had never scored above fifty runs in the cricket matches at his club. But the quiet resistance smote him badly. I now realise that. It made him dislike me even more.

It was a relief to be away at Sanawar during the school term and the next three years at Stephens College in Delhi. As soon as I had graduated, I decided that there was no way I was going to follow in his footsteps into the Indian Administrative or Allied Services and took the plunge into my first small business.'

Rene hugged him.

'I am so glad that you were one of those people who could find your way through all that baggage. That you did not let it stop you from achieving what you have, Jai,' she said.

'If anything, it spurred me on. Between setting up a business and attending evening classes for my MBA, I had no time to bear grudges. Or for chasing women, you know. Till now, that is.'

'That I don't believe, the no time for girls part, I mean,' laughed Rene. She peered up at his face to see that the bantering humour was back in place. It changed in a split second to passion at feeling her so close to him. A step towards each other was all it took to conclude the evening reasonably, if not completely satisfyingly for the two of them.

'Mmm. I wish you didn't have to go back to Dadi's tonight,' Jai sighed as they drove towards her temporary home.

'I wish,' she started and stopped herself, not knowing what exactly it was that she wished. She wanted very much to live in the moment but was wary of getting in too deep, worried that she may be already there. Instead, she continued,

'You said that your father had retired. And where is your brother, then?'

'Sandy is in Hong Kong at the moment. My half-brother and I are very close. He thinks I am some kind of a perfect creature,' laughed Jai. 'We are very good friends, actually. He joined me after he finished his education and is currently looking after our Hong Kong and Singapore offices. Dad and mum live in Dehradun, away from the pollution in Delhi. My actual father was in the merchant navy and died in a gas leak accident on board ship when my parents were on their extended honeymoon. I never knew him, really. When my grandparents discovered my mom was pregnant, they decided it best for mum to marry the younger son, as was not too uncommon in those days. So, dad is my uncle as well. Somewhat complicated, hmm?

But you know what, Rene, I've got over carrying the baggage of my younger days now. Now that I am so much older, I kind of understand where he was coming from. He was young and was pressured into marrying his brother's wife. Maybe he even had a girlfriend he wanted to marry; I don't know. All the same, he ended up loving my mother in the years that followed. I think he resented me because I was a constant reminder to him that he hadn't been the first man in my mother's life. You must be really confused trying to understand all the relationships involved.

And now here we are at Dadi's already. I'll see you tomorrow, around seven? Good night and sleep well, Dimpy. And promise to dream only of me?'

****

CHAPTER 22

A Request for Help

Uncle Rajan, meanwhile, had been trying hard through his police connections in the Indian Police Service to discover the whereabouts of Nimesha in Benares after they had had no luck in Delhi. They had through their slow, painstaking methods of search succeeded in locating three Rashmis and five Reshmas in Varanasi, as Benaras was now called, but none of them had heard of a Nimesha. They had drawn a blank. A dead end.

Jai picked Rene up on their way to dinner at the famous Karim's restaurant at Nizamuddin, not far from Dadi's house. Naina and Shweta were joining them as well. When they reached the whitewashed building with its red canopied windows, Rene's cousins were alighting from their car. The white uniformed and red peak-capped door keepers greeted them as they entered and the appetising smells of food assailed Rene's nose and her mouth was already watering as they took their seats.

According to Jai, the main restaurant in old Delhi was better, but Shweta thought otherwise. Jai had done a double take on seeing Shweta and announced to Rene,

'Your Nani's genes are very strong, I have to say. You could be sisters.' To which observation, Shweta replied with a giggle,

'We are. Well, first cousins, you know. Rene, you never said that he is so handsome. You make such an attractive couple.'

Jai raised his eyebrows at that and merely grinned wickedly. Naina looked surreptitiously at them both and smiled and nodded to herself, as if seeing something the others could not. She was, of course, an unusually perceptive girl and was hoping something would come of their friendship, if that was what it was. There was something about Rene that pulled at her and Naina realised with amazement how close she felt to her in this short time. She wished Rene would decide to live in India, here in Delhi.

They ordered burra kebab, a full leg of a goat called tandoori raan for entrée. Rene's nose twitched at the aroma.

'Oh my God, it smells divine! I don't think I've ever eaten this. Please, can we dig in?' she asked, forking a piece of the kebab. The others looked on in amusement, especially as her eyes rolled upwards, almost disappearing into her eyebrows.

She's so unpretentious, so different from the women I've known, thought Jai as he looked at her. Most of them would be picking at their food, eating daintily, however hungry they were. The mains followed – naans, roomali roti, a mixed vegetable dish, dal makhni, karahi gosht, a mutton curry and a chicken Mughlai. The meat was succulent, falling off the bone and was the best in the Mughal tradition of cooking. Rene had never tasted anything like that. For dessert, they had shahi tukda, another Mughlai delicacy. Translated, it meant royal morsel and was made of pieces of fried bread in thickened milk and nuts. It was rich, but delicious. Rene was shocked at how much she had eaten, purely from greed.

On the way home, though, Jai noticed that she looked pensive, especially when she thought he wasn't looking. With his usual perception where she was concerned, he remarked,

'What's up? You're worried about not getting anywhere with the search for Nimesha yet, aren't you? You have been very quiet since dinner.'

'Yes, I am feeling pretty discouraged. I was so hoping that the next step would be easier, especially now that we know where she went. But uncle Rajan has had no luck so far,' confessed Rene.

After dropping Rene off at Dadi's, Jai thought long and hard and arrived at a decision. It was not a very pleasant one as far as he was concerned, but if it would help Rene in some way, he would do it. Her hopelessness distressed him, more than he would admit. He made up his mind to call his father and ask for his help. His father still had his connections, and Jai knew that if anyone could find Nimesha, it would be his dad. Jai acknowledged that whatever else his dad wasn't, he was one of the best in his field.

The conversation Jai had that night with his parents puzzled him greatly. He sensed a strain in his mother's voice, but when he asked her if she was all right, she said,

'I'm just recovering from the flu, stop worrying.' His dad also sounded unusually subdued and not at all like his habitually superior self. He listened to what Jai had to say without interrupting once, which in itself was strange. When Jai had explained the situation to him, all he said was,

'I am happy you asked for my help, son. It is Yamini's nephew, after all. I will get on to it straight away.' Jai spent a long moment staring at the phone in his hand after hanging up.

True to his word, Jai's father was successful in receiving information about a fresh lead in Varanasi. This was the first indication of the whereabouts of Rashmi's dhera. As soon as Jai received the news, he called Rene and uncle Rajan.

Rene made her travel arrangements immediately and called her uncle Rajan to let him know. She called Naina before going, curious about her meeting with Rohit.

'Hi Naina, I am leaving with Jai tomorrow for Varanasi, so I thought I'd see if we could meet up before I leave. I don't know when I am likely to get back and, to be honest, I was also worried about how your meeting with Rohit went yesterday,' she said.

'Oh that! No surprises there, otherwise I would have called you. The only fresh development is that his family has kindly agreed to let me join their family garment business if I want to play at careers. I have complete respect for what they do to earn a living, and Rohit's sister is a very talented designer, but it is not something I have the remotest idea about. Neither is it something I want to do. In the end, it was like, you want to play; there are dolls, why do you want to go climb trees? Nothing has changed. But you were right; it was a relief to close the door on it finally. It is unfortunate, but both of us have to move on now. Anyway, how about joining us for dinner tonight? Mum's making goat's meat biryani, our favourite!'

Rene needed no urging after that. As soon as the cousins had settled down in Naina's room after eating enormous portions of the delicious biryani, Rani asked Naina,

'Are you seeing someone else? No nice guys at work?'

'You've got to be kidding! If my mom even hears a whisper of Naina didi having a boyfriend, she'll burst a blood vessel or something. Didi will probably have her marriage arranged for her, and that will be that. Especially after the episode with...,' Shweta stopped short and Rene intercepted a meaningful look pass from Naina to her younger sister. She didn't pursue it, deciding that it was a closed chapter now.

'I am not seeing anyone now, but I can't envisage going through an arranged marriage. But since I'm not in a relationship at the moment, there's no point getting into a discussion with mum until I have to,' replied Naina. She sounded very serious and firm in her decision.

Shweta choked on her apple juice. 'Discussion, she calls it! More like an all-out war. Anyway, papa is on her side, but he's told her that if she doesn't get hooked in the next two years, he won't be able to stop mom from doing her arranged *kanya daan* – giving away his daughter, you know,' Shweta announced, giving an exaggerated evil sounding laugh, avoiding a kick under the table from Naina as she did so.

'You're lucky though, aren't you, Rene? No one to put pressure on you to leap into a marriage with a total stranger, free to marry whoever you want, no caste this, religion that, state this etcetera, etcetera,' put in Naina.

'You're right. In that, an arranged marriage is not an option that I would consider even remotely. There are parents of some of my Indian friends, including Seema's, who have migrated from India and harbour some wishul thinking regarding arranged marriages for their kids. But they know that it's not realistic. And, while they worry that their son or daughter is getting older and not married or 'settled' as they call it, worrying and chatting about it endlessly with their friends, they know their children may not agree to even *meet* anyone they suggest. They will just keep their fingers crossed hoping their kids will find someone nice to share their lives with,' Rene replied.

Shweta was quite different from her sister. 'I don't know. I would be quite happy with an arranged marriage. Big deal, I don't think that some of Naina didi's married friends who had 'love marriages' look the picture of a happy married life exactly. Of course, I would like to meet the guy a few times and go out on dates before I get married. You know, not wait to hold hands looking for rings in the water,' she said.

'Rings in the water? What's *that* all about?'

Naina laughed. 'She's talking about an after the wedding ceremony where the bride and groom play some post ceremony games. One of them is where a ring is hidden by the groom's family in milky water and they look for the ring in it. Another is where they hold a cowrie shell tightly in their fist, while the partner tries to open it. The idea is whoever finds the ring first or keeps their fists closed the longest is going to be the dominant partner in the marriage. We think, though, that it was a sneaky way to allow the couple to touch each other – since in the old days, the couple didn't even know each other, let alone touch! Sometimes, they wouldn't even have seen each other before their wedding day!'

'Far out!' Rene exclaimed. 'Doesn't anybody date here?'

'Of course, they do! Some openly, many secretly. Some, maybe never. In many families still, we are not expected to have boyfriends or girlfriends, forget about going on dates. It is still the norm in most families to marry the person arranged for you by your parents. At the most, your parents will allow you to talk to your 'partner to be' in a chaperoned environment. Even after an engagement, you can talk on the phone and write to each other or go to movies in a group, that is, if you came from a progressive family. Even with many choosing to go for love marriages, especially in the metropolitan cities, men and women still have the option to enter into an arranged marriage, if they want. It's not considered weird or looked askance at, unlike in the West. My peers would probably shrug and say, oh well, whatever works,' Naina replied.

'True, if it works, it works. But where I live, I guess most of us fear that an arranged marriage, apart from being a weird concept, would probably look like a failure to have a relationship or inability to find someone yourself. An arranged marriage for me is simply too out there!' Rene laughed.

****

CHAPTER 23

A Funeral

'Rashmi died last night. How, you're asking? She got septic problem. The needle was infected. It was too late to do anything. Doctor said heart failed, kidneys failed. See, there are preparations being made for her cremation? Do you want to see? You want to know what time? Who told you it happens at night? Oho! I see you have the usual misconceptions about what happens when a kinnar dies. That we do our ceremonial preparations hidden from everyone, and bury or cremate in the dead of the night. Some of it is true, but not all, madamji. And we like to be called kinnars, not hijras.'

This was Tara, who was overseeing Rashmi's cremation. Her words were delivered in staccato form and shot out like bullets. Tara was fat, with skin the colour of unground wheat. There was a mean look about her eyes. She spat out a stream of red betel juice to her side, not caring whether she splattered anyone with it, and continued,

'I am going to be announced as the head of this house now. After Rashmi, I am the senior most kinnar, you see. As well as the most deserving, I'd say. But now we are busy. You come back the day after tomorrow. In the afternoon. Unless you want to come this afternoon for the cremation as well. Yes?' Then she burst out laughing, slapping her thighs and pinching another hijra called Revati, sitting next to her. 'Only a kinnar can attend the cremation, don't you know? How will you know, you are a memsahib!' With that, she continued with her raucous laughter.

Tara looked at Rene with her beady eyes and let out another crude cackle. She was waiting for the burial ceremony to be over so that she could take over as head of the dhera. She knew that most of the chelas hated her. They disliked her all the more because of the sharp contrast to Rashmi's gentle nature. But they also knew that she was tough and that the hard, peripheral world they lived in needed a leader who could be strong, even a little mean.

Revati, who clearly looked like a man wearing a woman's clothes, took pity on Rene and told her, 'You can attend Rashmiguru's cremation if you like. Normally, we don't allow anyone outside our community to attend except sometimes, someone from the dead kinnar's family. We ask the cremation or burial ground authorities to keep the ceremony a secret from non kinnars.'

She informed Rene that the cremation was going to be in the early afternoon, not during the night, and that she would try to convince Tara to let her come. Rene decided to attend Rashmi's cremation thinking it would soften the mean looking Tara towards her. She could sense that Tara would not be the helpful sort. Revati asked her to wait and after about fifteen minutes came back with a smile, saying that Rene could go provided that she wore pants and shirt like the rest of them.

'Rest of whom?' Rene asked.

'Us,' Revati replied. 'We will all go dressed as men so that nobody suspects that it is a kinnar's cremation taking place. This is what we do, normally.' she finished.

The last bit puzzled Rene, but since she was already wearing jeans and a kurta, she went to buy a shirt from the nearby shopping mall. She decided not to push her luck and ask too many questions just then.

****

When she came back Revati quickly pulled her to her side and into the middle of the procession before many of the others could get a good look at her.

Revati pushed a dark blue baseball type cap on Rene's head. 'Keep your head down,' she advised. There were many, many more mourners now than when Rene had left to go to the shops. Revati informed her they had come a few days before Rashmi had died in order to seek her blessings and pray for her soul.

'A kinnar who is on her deathbed is looked upon as godly and blessed with divine powers. If the kinnars come to know that one of us is dying, they travel from many parts of the country to seek the dying one's blessings,' Revati said.

Just as Revati had said, Rene saw that they were dressed either in a shirt and pants or kurta pajamas.

'They have come from far-off places to be here. As I said earlier, we dress like this so that people will not realise that the dead person is a kinnar,' explained Revati.

When the procession carrying Rashmi's body reached the burning ghat, Rene saw that someone had laid a funeral pyre made of wooden logs earlier on. Rashmi's body, wrapped in a clean white saree, was then laid on the pyre and Tara removed the jewellery and the red prayer strings around Rashmi's left hand.

Revati whispered, 'This is to cut off all ties the deceased had with the world of the living. Now she can travel peacefully into the next world. We pray for her to be born either as a complete man or woman in her next birth.

Rashmiguru is being cremated because she was a Hindu. Not all kinnars are buried, as many people think. Only Muslims are buried. We have many beliefs regarding this last rite of ours, you know. Some believe that the soul will escape and enter the body of a non kinnar and he will be born as a kinnar in the next life. When one of our Muslim sisters dies, we usually bury them deep under the ground, preferably covered with large stones. We believe that, in this way, it will be too hard for their souls to escape from their bodies and condemn other lives, thus saving them from this cursed life of ours.'

Holy water, taken from the river Ganges, was then poured into Rashmi's mouth, after which Tara set the pyre alight. Everyone present folded their hands in prayer. As they left the ghat, Revati informed Rene that normally they would have invited a male relative of Rashmiguru to perform the last rites but that unfortunately she had no living relatives, male or otherwise.

'So, as Tara is the senior most kinnar in our family, she is allowed to perform the rites.' added Revati.

'Who pays for the funeral costs?' asked Rene.

'We do. We are poor, but we all chip in and do our bit to raise the money,' answered Revati, showing off her newfound knowledge of western slang.

Revati had finished her high school board exams in Haryana before she had run away from a middle class home. Her father was a security guard at a bank and beat her mercilessly, breaking one of her wrists when he found her cross dressing one day. He had threatened to bring his gun home and shoot her if he ever found her doing it again. Revati had not doubted that he would do exactly that. Her mother was also a victim of her husband's violence and was too scared of him to protect her only child. So one day, when her mother was having an afternoon nap and her father was at work, Revati, then Rajat, stole money from her father's drawer and a gold chain belonging to her mother from her almirah, and took the train to Varanasi.

'I have been here since then. Rashmiguru was very nice to me and helped me to settle down quickly. I had wanted to study further, but I didn't know how. Finding time to do anything but earn my living was hard. I've been too busy trying to earn money dancing at weddings and births so that I can stay off prostitution. I hate the way people look at us when we go to perform badhai, to bless newborn children. That look of barely concealed loathing. People just about tolerate us. Or they fear us. But for the most part, we are invisible. We are not a part of the regular sphere of anyone's lives, whether it is socially, at work or in educational institutions. Just some grotesque half man, half woman. Even gays and lesbians have their small niche in high society, but they are still gender identifiable. Recently, we have been given the newly introduced *adhar* or identity card but we have no *adhar*, really. We may be officially given the tag of a third gender but for the society at large we don't really exist, except as a nuisance,' Revati said.

Rene was very thoughtful and filled with sadness as she went back to her hotel that evening. She thought that Revati's words must echo Nimesha's, and it took her a while to get to sleep.

****

CHAPTER 24

Regrets

At about three in the afternoon, Rene received a call from Jai from his hotel room. He had been on business calls all morning and announced that he was leaving for Dehradun as soon as he could get a flight. She was a bit puzzled and curious too and asked him why he was leaving so suddenly when there had been no plans the night before.

'I think something's wrong. My mother called just now. Her voice sounded strange, panicked almost. I think she's been hiding something from me. I have been suspecting for a few days that she's not well or something. She's always been very good at pulling the wool over my eyes every time she's been unwell. Once she had fractured her wrist in a road accident and didn't let me know until she was well on the road to recovery. She's keeping something from me, I'm certain of that. But what's scaring me more is that she has asked me to come to Dehradun. I don't want to leave you here by yourself either.' Jai sounded panicked himself.

'Calm down,' advised Rene. 'You're not likely to be of any help to anyone like this, anyway. Just go. And don't work yourself up imagining all sorts of negative stuff. Call me when you get there, please. Anyway, there's nothing happening today. I haven't much to do other than wait for Revati to call me with further information. Besides, Shweta's school holidays have begun and she and Naina are joining me tomorrow. I am sure everything will be all right.' 'I hope it's nothing serious,' she finished softly to herself, looking thoughtful.

The last flight to Dehradun had left from Varanasi, but Jai managed a seat on one flying to Delhi. Bhola was waiting at the airport and the two left immediately for Dehradun in the car.

Jai asked the driver to drive non-stop with only a short tea break on the way. Normally, he loved watching the beautiful scenery and the hills, but today he was unaware of the beauty of his surroundings, so engrossed was he with worry about his mother.

Jai jumped out of the car the second it stopped in front of the long veranda. When his mother opened the door to his ringing of the doorbell, he was only slightly reassured. His mother hugged him tightly and tears rolled down her thin cheeks.

'Jai! Oh God, I am so glad you're here at last. He's been asking for you,' she said.

'Are you all right, Mom? And who's been asking for me?' Jai asked worriedly. At the same time, the penny dropped. 'Dad?' he asked. 'What's wrong Mom? Don't cry please. What's the matter? Tell me!' he exclaimed, his voice shaking with worry.

Jai's dad had been diagnosed with pancreatic cancer about three weeks ago and had not wanted his sons to be told just yet. He had asked his wife to wait until the surgery was scheduled to let them know.

'When's the surgery, then?' asked Jai, shocked and worried at the news.

'That's the worst part. When they did the CT scan, the cancer had spread to the liver, and the tumour is in a place which makes surgery not an option anymore. So the doctors have advised chemotherapy at this stage. He's in the hospital for the first one, which is happening tomorrow morning. It was such a struggle to get him to agree to that. You know how stubborn he can be.' And she burst into tears, the tension of the last few weeks finding release at last in her son's arms.

Jai and his mother left straightaway for the hospital. When he entered his father's room, it shocked Jai to see him looking so thin and frail. He had always been a tall, stocky man but now looked shrunken, lying on the hospital bed. Jai stood looking down at his father, not knowing what to say to him. For so long there had been no love lost between the two of them, but looking at him now, Jai could only feel a deep sadness. He did not know why. Whether it was for the wasted years or his father's physical deterioration, he could not say.

After speaking to his father for a little while, and having no recollection of the words he spoke, Jai went to find the oncologist. On enquiring about the prognosis, Jai was extremely disturbed to be informed that his father had a year to live at best. Jai went to the little green area called the Healing Garden and sat there on a bench, surprised to find his eyes wet. He rubbed his hands together and clenched and unclenched his hands a few times, as if that would help clarify the strange emotions running through his heart. Regret, sadness, he had expected to feel, but he was feeling something far more painful, a grief that was unfamiliar, something he had not expected and, therefore, could not understand.

His mother came to find him. 'There you are. I see that his doctor has told you. I could not face it alone, so I called you. Sandy has also just arrived. He is with your father now,' she said.

Sandy looked up when they walked into the room and there was the same shock reflected in his eyes at his father's condition. After a while, Jai motioned with his head to Sandy to step out of the room. Jai informed Sandy about the doctor's prognosis and the brothers sat outside the room with Jai's arm around his younger brother's shoulders. Sandy's shoulders heaved suspiciously, as if he was crying, and Jai could only give his shoulders a tight squeeze as he saw his mother coming out of the room.

Looking at Jai, she said, 'He is asking for you again. He wants to talk to you alone,' said his mother. So saying, she went quietly towards the waiting lounge, signaling Sandy to follow her.

Jai went back into his father's cabin and stood by his bed. His father indicated the chair on the right side of his bed for Jai to sit near him, close to his head.

He said nothing for a space, perhaps thinking of how to put his thoughts into words. After a while he turned towards Jai and there was desperation, a pleading in his eyes.

****

Later, when Jai spoke to Rene about his trip, he said,

'He didn't say a word at first. There was just that look in his eyes that said it all. He held my hand, and it was the pleading and the regret in his eyes that shook me. I could tell that it was my forgiveness he was asking, as if he had actually said the words. I have never felt so small in my life!'

'When he spoke at last, he said something that confirmed what I had thought.' continued Jai.

'What did he say?' questioned Rene.

Jai's eyes were troubled. Worry curled his stomach. His voice shook a little.

'Dad said,

"I wanted to ask you something, Jai. Don't say no. When I die, I want you to do my last rites, beta."

As he said this, a single tear ran down the side of his eye and his grip on my hand tightened slightly. Oh God, I really want him to live, Rene. He should have years more to go. Not *so* soon. Can I ask you something? I will leave for Dehradun, probably next week. Rene, will you go with me? I am sure he would like to meet you.'

'Of course, I will. Have you thought of what's going to happen when Sandy goes back, though? Your mom needs one of you with her to see this through, right?'

'Yes, I have been thinking of that and am trying to get an appointment for the remaining sessions of his chemotherapy in Delhi. That way, I can be around all the time,' answered Jai.

****

During the next week, Jai was busy making arrangements for his parents' move to Delhi in consultation with his father's doctor. Rene informed Revati and left for Delhi. She accompanied Jai to Dehradun to bring his parents back and tried to make the nearly six-hour journey less tedious and fun by trying to read the hilarious messages on the backs of some of the trucks with her anglicized Hindi pronunciation and a million mistakes.

During the visit, Rene was glad that her presence lightened the atmosphere for everyone. Jai's dad assured her he would do his best to help her find Nimesha despite his illness and Rene found that extremely touching. Jai's mother also remembered her from her childhood and shared some interesting and happy memories of Rene's mother with her; and in between talking and getting everything ready for the trip back, there was not much time to think about what the future held.

****

CHAPTER 25

Varanasi

On her return to Varanasi, Naina and Shweta accompanied Rene. Uncle Rajan had booked a 'surprise' hotel for them, details of which he refused to divulge. He was enjoying himself after a long time, indulging the three girls as much as his staid personality would allow.

Some of the hotel staff received them at the airport and they were taken in a car to one *ghat* on the banks of the river Ganges, called Bhisasur Ghat. Puzzled, the girls looked around but could not see anything that looked like a hotel. They were soon, however, escorted into a *bajra*, a traditional Indian boat. The ride was not a very long one and Rene eagerly soaked in the atmosphere. It was all so different from what she was used to. As the boat slowed and made its way to another famous ghat called Darbhanga Ghat, Shweta gasped in awe. Rene had been looking the other way, and she turned at the sound, staring in wonder at the beautiful palace arising almost from the water itself.

The hotel staff informed them that they had arrived at the hotel Brijrama Palace. Shweta's uninhibited expressions of excitement and joy were met with broad grins. The two older girls just stared in awe.

Built in the Maratha architectural style in 1812, the erstwhile palace was one of the oldest landmarks of Varanasi. The majestic sandstone walls and beautiful pillars rose gracefully from a series of steps leading down into the water. The palace had been lovingly restored and had become one of the most sought after hotels, although it was quite expensive as hotels went. At either extreme of the palace, near the top, there was a semicircular bastion with a prismatic turret in the centre. As the boatman tied the boat to its moorings, Rene could see that here and there people had already started placing clay lamps filled with oil on the steps, ready to be lit as dusk fell.

A hotel employee guided them to an elevator.

'It is the first elevator built in India in 1918,' she informed them proudly. Hearing this, the girls looked at it a little doubtfully, but it worked perfectly and took them to their second-floor room without mishap.

Uncle Rajan had booked a special suite for the girls. It was very spacious, with huge four poster beds and comfortable looking settees. Hand painted art adorned the walls. The cushions, curtains and bedspreads were all furnished ornately with the famous Banarasi silk. Here and there, brass lamps adorned the tables. The bathroom was luxurious and Shweta immediately decided to soak herself in the claw footed bathtub. The room had one of the semicircular bastions which held a sitting area affording a wonderful view of the Ganges.

After taking a tour of the suite, 'I feel quite like royalty!' Rene exclaimed.

They had to pull Shweta out of the tub to be on time for their afternoon tea. The girls went up to the terrace café, where they had an uninterrupted view of the river. There was a sumptuous array of snacks and cakes, which all three girls pigged on guiltlessly.

Rene called Jai after their tea and he brought her up to date on how his parents were settling in after their move. He sounded a little more relaxed now that they were living with him. The doctors had seen his dad and they would resume the rest of his treatment a week later, Jai informed her.

****

As twilight set in, the girls were taken on a complimentary boat ride by the hotel boatman to Dashashwamedh Ghat to witness the Ganga Aarti, a ritual to invoke the blessings of Lord Shiva using ghee lamps.

'Eighty-four ghats line the eight kilometre long Ganga River, but this ghat is the most famous because of this ritual. It is so called because Lord Brahma sacrificed ten horses during Dasa-Ashvamedha yajna performed here,' the boatman informed them.

They had arrived early enough to get a front row view of the ritual. Even as their boat took its place among the early visitors, the spaces behind started filling up quickly. Most of the balconies and available spaces above the ghat were full within minutes.

A group of young priests wearing orange robes performed the ritual on a series of stages along the ghat. There were trays of flowers and other prayer articles in front of each. The smell of sandalwood incense hung heavy in the air. The aarti commenced with the synchronized blowing of conch shells. This was followed by the priests circling flaming lamps and incense sticks in elaborate patterns in time with the rhythmic chanting of hymns and the ringing of hand held bells. It was a beautiful sight, all the priests moving in tandem, the lamps lighting up the sky over the magnificent river. Afterwards Rene wrote in her email to Helen and Seema,

'Although I found it somewhat staged, the entire experience was very uplifting and sensory, one of the most awe inspiring sights I've ever seen. I wish you two could have been here.'

****

Rene and the girls had dinner at their hotel in *chota angan* which translated to small courtyard. It was a pretty, candle lit place with intricate glasswork and blue and silver Thikri art on the walls. After dinner, the girls sat in the semicircular window in their room, looking out at the river and watching the lamps floating on the water, cast by people thronging the ghats.

After much deliberation, the girls planned to take the sunrise boat tour on their first morning, which Rene later thought was the highlight of their visit to Varanasi.

Although Shweta grumbled the most about having to wake up at the crack of dawn, she was also the most excited at watching the sun rise over the calm river. As the row boat glided slowly along the gently moving waters of the Ganges, they saw some beautiful former palaces and some of the ghats along the banks on either side in the rosy glow of the rising sun. Rene let the spiritual charm of the journey seep into her senses and she felt mentally relaxed after a long time. For those few hours she felt the anxiety that the search for Nimesha had caused, leave her body.

Shweta coaxed Rene into eating the famous *kachori sabzi* and the sweet *rabri* of Varanasi for breakfast at a small street café. The food was mouth wateringly tasty but Rene fully expected her stomach to revolt during the day.

After breakfast, they visited the famous Kashi Vishwanath and Durga temples. The hotel guide took them through narrow alleyways, dodging people, scooters, cows and rickshaws – to where the silk weavers lived and worked. Rene was amazed at the way they managed to navigate the narrow lanes. It seemed as if the sides of the rickshaws touched the walls on either side. Rene bought sarees for Sudha mami, Yamini bua and on impulse, one for herself. Naina refused to accept one saying that she hardly ever wore sarees and had too many of them already. Réne also bought some cushion covers for her friends.

They took their purchases and headed back to the hotel for lunch. Just as they sat down to lunch, Rene received a call from Revati.

'There is a wedding tonight very close to Darbhanga ghat. We are going to perform badhai there. I heard there are two other hijra groups attending as well. This might be your chance to see if your sister is there or get some more information,' she informed Rene. 'Oh, and take some money with you. No canary will sing without that,' she laughed.

Revati gave directions and the address to the wedding venue, which was right behind their hotel. Naina and Shweta opted to stay at the hotel to watch a movie in their room while Rene was away.

****

Revati met Rene at the entrance to the gateway of the wedding venue. When she walked in, she saw to her surprise that it was actually a group wedding. There were six brides on one side of the rectangular hall, where already some hijras were performing a haphazardly put together dance while a few sang, accompanied by a man playing the harmonium. The gestures were an exaggerated parody of a woman's mannerisms.

'Our singing and dancing invoke blessings on the newlyweds for fertility. We are also bestowed with the power of blessing newborn children with long lives and prosperity,' explained Revati earnestly.

As they finished their dance, Revati led Rene to one of the kinnars who appeared to be in charge of the group. She quickly asked some questions but got only a blank stare in response. She whispered to Rene and waved a hundred rupee note Rene gave her. The group leader was silent, but she was definitely taking in Rene's presence and appearance from the periphery of her vision.

'Give me your number,' she spoke directly to Rene. 'If I hear something, I'll call you,' she added and, before she could react, plucked the hundred rupee note out of Revati's hand. Revati reached to snatch it back, but Rene laid a hand on her arm and stopped her. She gave Revati some money for her trouble and waited for the other groups to come.

By this time Revati had surmised that none of the other group members had ever heard of Nimesha. Meanwhile, her own group members were ready, and they performed a very well-choreographed dance accompanied by music on a CD player. The bridal party handed money over, after which the group made their way to the grooms' side of the hall.

Two more groups came and performed badhai but none of them had heard of Nimesha either. Rene looked carefully at each one of them to see if one of them could be her sister, but none of the faces gave her that feeling. In the end, she returned to the hotel feeling quite dejected.

Rene accompanied Revati to three more weddings and a celebration of the birth of a baby boy. One evening, Jai arrived unannounced for a flying visit to Varanasi. As they walked down the banks of the river under the darkening sky, Jai whispered in Rene's ear, 'I really came because I missed you. How do you Aussies say it? Heaps!'

Later, Rene sat with her head on Jai's shoulder on the steps leading down to the river, her face looking happy in the flickering light of the tiny lamps. She did not know what lay in the future for them, but for now, she was content to let things ride.

Jai accompanied Rene and Revati to the last of the weddings. In hindsight, it was both a good and a bad decision. Revati had had to leave to attend another event shortly after her group's performance. As Jai and Rene were leaving the venue, a stout kinnar from another group approached Jai and lunged suggestively at him. Jai pushed her away, but she was big and muscular and pinned Jai to the wall behind him, nearly molesting him. She had reached for his trouser button when suddenly, the leader of the group appeared and angrily shoved the perpetrator away, giving her a stinging slap in the face. As Rene looked at her, she realised it was the same person to whom she had given her number at the first wedding. The leader introduced herself as Mithali and when she saw Jai reach for his phone, pleaded with him not to report the incident.

'I am asking you to forgive us on her behalf. We are not all like this. We are maligned because of a few black sheep like this bitch here. Our entire group will suffer at the hands of the police if you complain. You can be sure we will punish her when we go back. All her heat will dissipate in no time!'

Jai agreed to drop the matter and Rene thanked Mithali for intervening before they made their way back to the hotel.

****

CHAPTER 26

Mithali Helps

Mithali finally broke her silence. Two days after Jai had left, Rene received a call from an unknown number. She and the girls were taking in some more of the sights and sounds of Varanasi, walking in the little gullies and food lanes of the city, shopping and eating. They had stopped at a street café selling hot jalebis dipped in milk, served in a bowl made of dried sal leaves, stitched together with needle thin grass sticks. The call came as they were having steaming hot tea spiced with cardamom and cinnamon.

'I am Mithali. You remember me? At the group wedding you gave me your number? You asked me if I knew anything about your sister. I think I may have some news for you.'

'Yes, I remember you and your intervention the other day too.' Rene glanced up at the café sign for the street name. 'Can you meet me now?' When Mithali agreed, she gave her the address of the café.

Rene waited for Mithali with little hope. She was probably just trying to get more money out of her, Rene thought.

Mithali arrived in about fifteen minutes and Rene ordered tea and jalebis for her as well. People sitting nearby either gawked curiously or openly shocked to see such an unlikely group sitting together at the café. After hastily finishing the jalebis, Mithali said,

'Your sister is in Mumbai. I asked around our dhera and other community members soon after the first time we met – at that first wedding. I knew soon after I saw you that first time, but I didn't want to give you the information. Why should I make things easy for you, I thought. Then again, I thought you were kind enough to cooperate with us in not reporting the incident to the police, so I decided why not?'

Rene waited with bated breath. She felt somehow that she was finally getting somewhere; her sixth sense giving her goose bumps all over her arms. She wished Mithali would get to the point quickly instead of adding the entire preamble.

'It appears your sister is well known in Mumbai. However, you will need to contact Ramaguru to help you find her. I cannot guarantee that she will. Help you, I mean. Nimesha is her name, and she is definitely in Mumbai, that much is certain. I don't have her address though,' said Mithali and handed Rene a tiny slip of paper with the name Ramaguru printed on it. She remained sitting expectantly and although the city and name alone were not a lot to go on with, Rene fished out a five hundred rupee note and when Mithali looked askance at that, added another.

Mithali's face lit up with a smile as she took the money and she left quickly after that, hailing a rickshaw as she walked away.

The next day Rene, Naina and Shweta returned to Delhi and Rene stayed over at their house for the night. Uncle Rajan was pleased that finally things were looking up for Rene, but wisely did not pass on the information to his wife Sudha. He did not want to press his luck just yet.

****

The next evening, Nani and Nana arrived in Delhi, ostensibly to visit their son's family, but really to spend as much time as they could with Rene. The next few days saw Rene the happiest she had been in days, cocooned in the love of her grandparents and cousins. Upon Jai's invitation, the cousins and her aunt and uncle accompanied Rene to Jai's house. Nani and Nana begged off, not used to late nights. Jai's dad was happy that Nimesha's whereabouts, or at least the city she was in, were known now. Rene was pleasantly surprised to see Yamini bua already there. Sandeep, Jai's brother, was there too, making a merry party.

Other than being of the same height, Sandy and Jai did not share any physical resemblance. Sandeep was of a stockier built and had a squarish, good looking face with a little goatee on his chin. His eyes danced with a very mischievous look, and he broke into a smile at the slightest opportunity.

Jai's father was handling his treatment really well. Apart from a controlled diet, nothing much had changed for him. He went for his walks regularly and, according to Jai, seemed more relaxed than when he had first started his treatment. He took the slip of paper from Rene and promised to help find Ramaguru's address for her.

Sandy and Shweta got on famously. Rene, however, caught Naina rolling her eyes more than once. For most of the evening, Naina ignored Sandy completely. When Rene confronted her with it later, Naina simply shrugged her shoulders and said,

'I don't know. Bit of a know it all type. Offered to 'help' with starting an NGO by trying to give a donation. Throwing his money around, basically.'

'Come on Naina, he seems to be such an easy-going kind of guy. Don't be so judgemental! Give him a break,' Rene scoffed. She found it funny the way she had neatly stepped into a big sister role.

Dinner was a simple but delicious meal of goat meat biryani, yoghurt raita, stuffed okra and a potato salad that Jai had put together.

****

Three days later Jai came over and excitedly gave the news she had been waiting to hear. He bounded through Dadi's front door and announced,

'Guess what, babe? Dad's contact has unearthed Ramaguru's whereabouts. In fact, he has her address in Mumbai. I'll organise the tickets immediately. Since Sandy's here for a few days and tomorrow happens to be a Friday, I'll be able to go with you too and stay till the weekend.' He appeared as excited as she was, at this good turn in their luck.

Dadi smiled to see their happiness and was glad that finally a ray of hope seemed to have come their way.

****

The next day Dadi found Rene sitting on Dadi's broad jhoola, swinging gently and lost in thought, staring at nothing in particular, a small smile playing about her lips. Dadi had walked in after her morning prayers in her courtyard and stood there gazing at Rene with a little smile of her own.

'What are you thinking, beta? Although I think I can make a good guess,' she remarked.

'I think I am in love, Dadi,' blurted Rene.

Dadi just looked at her with her eyebrows raised and an impudent grin lit up her face, making her look quite young right then.

'What?' queried Rene, with an answering smile.

'Are you sure it is love? After all, ninety percent of the 'love' in a relationship is made up of lust, isn't it?' Dadi asked.

'Dadi! I am shocked! How can you be so cynical? As it is, I am in so much self-doubt and you're not helping at all. And you were the one all set on matchmaking with Jai even as soon as you met him,' Rene protested.

'All that is fine if you go into a marriage or relationship, as you young people call it – with your eyes open. As long as you don't have expectations of the undying love of romantic novels. But I have observed you Rene, in the past few months. You want it all. The romance, the lust and tenderness, which is sometimes a huge ask, you know,' Dadi answered.

Rene's expression confirmed that what Dadi said was a hundred percent true.

Dadi continued, 'and I am not being cynical or trying to second guess your feelings, child. I was lucky in my marriage. In the first years we argued, loved, and fought, all of that. I had quite a temper, you know. Once I even threw a bunch of boiled spinach leaves at my husband in anger, spoiling his white shirt forever. Fortunately, they were just warm, not boiling hot.'

'Dadi! You didn't! I can't even *imagine* you doing that!' laughed Rene.

'I did too! But both of us loved each other and, more important than that, we respected each other. Then I fell ill and had my uterus, ovaries and breasts removed. The lust part of our relationship became almost non-existent.' Dadi's eyes filled with tears.

'Shantanu, my husband never once let me feel that there was any change in our relationship, our love for each other. He became even more caring and protective. That was when I understood that what we had *was* love,' she reminisced.

'From what I have seen, Jai is a wonderful boy. He probably is as much in love with you as you are with him. In fact, if I was to bet, I would put my money on it. But how would it work? Would you be willing to move to India to live with him here? Could he leave his businesses or run them long distance from Australia? My feeling is that you probably need to think through all of this before you commit your heart completely, beta. If it's not too late,' advised Dadi gently.

****

CHAPTER 27

An Address

Ramaguru was as different from Sumati and Tara as it was possible to be. For one thing, unlike Sumati, there was nothing remotely gentle about her. She was loud, she was coarse, and she was very ugly. Everything was overdone about her. She had on a thick layer of make-up, many shades too light for her dark skin, and it stood out in patches. Dark rouge on her cheeks gave her a clownish appearance. Huge earrings dangled from her large ears and at least a dozen bangles adorned her thick wrists.

She had on a bright red saree and wore heavy, multi coloured jewellery around her neck that looked terribly garish. Her mannerisms were exaggerated, from the typical hand clapping style adopted by the kinnars to the exaggerated feminine gestures trying to mask her masculine looks. However, underneath the ugliness and outward crudity, she had a good heart, unlike Tara.

'*Badi chikni ho. Tu to yahan ki nahin lagti? Tu bhi kitna chikna hai,*' Ramaguru laughed. Roughly translated later by Jai, it meant, 'you are very pretty, you don't seem to be from hereabouts. *You* are very cute too.' The last bit was aimed at Jai.

'Yes,' said one of her chelas with a bawdy laugh! She touched first Rene's and then Jai's cheek and asked him,

'How smooth your skin feels. Don't you find me more attractive? Is she your lagau, your wife?'

Rene tried not to flinch at the sudden touch, but Ramaguru shouted at the chela,

'Get out of here, you shameless hussy! She never loses an opportunity to attach herself to any male she sees. Move, get away and do your housework, you lazy bitch!'

The chela moved away sulkily with a belligerent glance thrown at Rene and Jai.

'We are happy to pay for any information that will help us,' said Jai, taking out his wallet.

Ramaguru looked at the roll of money in Jai's hands and only the gleam in her eyes told them that she needed the money desperately. Rene and Jai both thought that her pretence at dignity was very sad, and Rene felt a wave of pity.

'You can't buy us with money, you know,' Ramaguru said as if reading their thoughts. 'We too have self-respect. We will beg, steal, even prostitute ourselves, but we will not sell out one of our own.' She took out a *bidi*, rolled it between her hands and lit it with a match before putting it between her thick lips. After a few puffs, she shook the ash on to the ground to her side.

'Why should we? We have to protect our own from the vultures ready to pounce on us,' she continued, more to herself than to Rene.

Rene looked crestfallen and was beginning to lose hope that they could find any breakthrough in her search for her brother. She turned away and gestured to Jai, shrugging her shoulders somewhat dejectedly.

'But I didn't say I won't help you,' came Ramaguru's voice behind her back. 'You accepted defeat so soon? Come inside for a few minutes and I will see what I can help you with.'

Ramaguru led them to the first floor of a ramshackle, old, two storey building. It had probably once been whitewashed, but was now a dull grey with blue streaks formed by the indigo mixed with lime.

The windows were broken and had been patched and boarded crudely in places, while the curtains fluttering in the humid breeze had seen better days. The steps were narrow, made of concrete, bits of which had chipped off here and there. There was no railing to hold on to and Rene had to hang on to Jai's arm to keep from tripping.

They entered a room with the barest of furnishings. One string bed with a thin mattress, more like a bedspread, was pushed against one wall. There was no pillow. A large picture of a God or Goddess of some sort was the only form of decoration in the room. Ramaguru saw Rene looking and said,

'That is Bahuchara Mata. All kinnars pray to her. She is our patron goddess. Come here, sit down. Let me look at you. There is *something* about you that urges me to help you. But before I do that, I need to have more details,' she continued as she squatted cross-legged on the string bed. Rene sat on the only chair in the room, while Jai stood near the door.

'Why are you looking for Nimesha?' she asked.

'He is my brother, or sister now, and I did not know that she existed until a month or so ago,' replied Rene honestly, and described to Ramaguru just how she had found out.

Ramaguru looked seriously at her. 'Do you understand that Nimesha may not want to be found by you?' she said gravely. 'Of what use will it be to her to meet you? It may only bring her sadness again, memories of what she must have suffered, those that caused her to run away from home in the first place.'

'I was only a child then,' interjected Rene. 'I have done nothing wrong. If you would only take me to her, I am sure she would not refuse to see me. I will not pester her or anything. If after that she does not want to meet me, or indicates that she does not want to have anything to do with me, I will respect that. I will go back home, knowing that she is alive and safe, at the very least.'

'All right, then. Let me sleep on it. You come back tomorrow morning at ten o'clock. I will let you know my decision after talking to my dadaguru. I have to consult her first. But I will do my best to convince her. That is why I wanted to find out your intentions. We don't give out information about anyone in our community without good reason, if at all,' she added as she saw them off at the door.

****

The next morning, Rene went alone in an auto rickshaw from the hotel. The driver was very curious about her destination, but refrained from asking with a lot of difficulty. She asked him to wait for her with the promise of a hefty tip.

Ramaguru was waiting for her with a note in her hand. She gave it to Rene, saying,

'This is the address. We have decided to help you for two reasons. One because I felt you would find her anyway, today or tomorrow. She is very well known in Mumbai and her name is Nimesha. But the real reason is that both dadaguru and I like you. We feel you seem to be a good person. You have come so far to find your sister; we should not disappoint you. Mata would be angry with us. I called you to my home because dadaguru wanted to listen to you through the lattice ventilator up in the wall over there, from her room next door.'

Rene stared at the paper in her hands with a mixture of gladness and fear of the unknown. Uncertainty about the outcome of her meeting with her lost sibling held her in its grip. Thanking Ramaguru, she left, wondering what was in store for her.

CHAPTER 28

Nimesha's Story

The staircase was narrow, if clean. A red net scarf with gold tassels was tied to one of the stair rails. As Rene glanced upwards, she saw a kinnar standing at the top of the stairs.

She had folded her hands together in the traditional namaste pose. Her clothes were terribly garish. A bright yellow salwar suit with a candy pink dupatta, shot with bright gold flowers. On her face lipstick formed an awkward slash of red and her cheeks were heavily rouged. Rene's heart sank as she looked at her.

Then her gaze shifted to another woman behind the first, slightly to her left. She was tall, dressed simply in a pale blue saree, her hair coiled in a loose bun behind her head. She wore a small nose stud and a matching pair of bigger studs in her ears. A pale rose lipstick adorned her fair face and a thin line of kohl lined her eyes, and that was all. In her hands she was holding what looked like a silver, maybe steel, plate. In it was a small oil lamp, its dancing flame throwing light on some marigold flowers scattered on the plate.

But Rene was beyond noticing anything anymore. Her gaze became transfixed on the second woman's face, and all sights and sounds merged into a strange stillness. She knew without a doubt that this was her brother, her sister, the sight of whom was a joyful culmination of her emotional and physical journeys so far. She looked longingly at this beautiful creature. It was like looking at an older version of her own self. No, that was not quite true. The face that she gazed at was far more stunning, the cheekbones a little more prominent. The temples also jutted out a little. She could have been a model, a film star, she was so beautiful. However, the eyes were the same dark brown, the expression in them still as gentle as she remembered from the photograph.

****

Nimesha looked at her sister with mixed feelings. A peculiar mixture of joy and pride that this beautiful woman was her little sister, and hesitation mingled with doubt that they would have any connection with each other after all these years. She searched in herself for some feelings of jealousy, some resentment perhaps, that Tarini here was a complete woman, that she had had all the advantages that her family could have given her, while she herself had lived the life of an outcast, seen by society as half man, half woman or neither. But all she could feel were the tears welling up in her eyes, the squeezing of her heart that told her to hold her sister to her bosom, much as she had done when Rene had been just a baby. She felt disbelief that the baby was now grown up and had come looking for her after all this time.

Even as she hesitated, Rene took the steps that breached the distances of time and borders and, holding her older sibling's arms, said,

'I am your sister. You are mine. Please don't send me away. Do you know, all these years, you have never been far from me? I have been seeing you in my dreams till now, but I must have always known you were there, somewhere.'

Nimesha started crying with great heaving sobs as Rene spoke and folded her in her embrace. Their tears mingled and flowed. She rocked back and forth, as if quietening a small child, crying as if the tears would wash away the sands of time and all the heartache that had been her life so far. She looked with wonder at her sister, who was so much like her, yet so utterly different.

The past crowded into her mind, and the present blurred with her painful memories.

****

Nimesha had been seven years old for a week when her mother had come home from the hospital, carrying the new baby in her arms. She had been a boy then and his grandmother had named him Nimesh. He, as she was then, had insisted on being allowed to hold the baby in his arms. His face gleaming with excitement, he sat cross-legged on the bed and the baby was given to him to hold in his lap. Nimesh had loved his little sister on sight. He was not allowed to visit the baby in the hospital because he had not been well. Even then, he had not felt threatened or jealous of his sibling's arrival. After all, he had been begging his mother to 'buy' a baby from the hospital ever since he could remember.

Whenever he could, Nimesh helped his mother change the baby's nappies, give her a bath or at least shower baby powder all over her. Most times, a song sung in his childish voice would quieten the baby, even lull her to sleep. He was a little mother, except in pants. Ma used to be amused and grateful for the respite from sleeplessness, but Dadi used to chase him away, saying that it was not boys' work.

As Rene grew up, she adored her brother. There were times when she became very confused whether she had a sister or a brother because of the way Nimesh had dressed sometimes. He dressed in girls' clothes in secret, or when they had played together by themselves in their room. Mana, the ayah's daughter, would lend him her clothes. Nimesh had sworn her to secrecy with bribes of lollies, toys, boiled eggs and assorted snacks, given to her wrapped in newspapers, hidden from prying eyes. Nimesh loved helping his mother in the kitchen, and his concern touched her. However, the ayah had never lost a chance to make fun of him when he had done so.

Nimesh's childhood had been mostly happy till he started middle school, at about the age of ten. He had begun to sense that there was something different about him. His tastes differed from other boys. He took no interest in the games that they played, did not like football, flying kites, wading through ponds to catch frogs – activities that his class fellows seem to enjoy. Nimesh gazed longingly at the girls skipping, playing hopscotch or the various hand clapping games they played during recess. He started to hate his male clothes. He wished he could wear frocks or the long, mirror worked skirts some girls he knew wore.

Once he had ventured to ask a group of girls whether he could join them during playtime. They had hooted with laughter at his tentative suggestion and had giggled whenever he had passed them ever since.

Soon, the boys started noticing that he preferred to sit by himself instead of playing with them, sometimes knitting a garment for the doll he had asked Nani to buy for him, sometimes reading. Once in a while, they would see him skipping by himself.

It was not long before he became a laughing stock in the school and he was at a loss to know why. He was only doing what he loved and enjoyed, so why was everyone making fun of him, he wondered.

It did not take long before the teachers also heard about the strange behaviour of this otherwise bright boy. They discussed the matter with the principal, who called his parents. Nimesha remembered sitting in the principal's room and the conversation clearly.

Mr. Tarapore, the principal waved his parents to some very rickety looking chairs and, with little in the way of an introduction, said,

'Mr. and Mrs. Ray Chowdhury, I have called you here to discuss your son's strange behaviour at school recently.'

'Oh! Isn't he studying well? I thought he was doing well?' Ma interposed uncertainly.

'No, no, it is not about his studies.' He fished out a report card. 'Let me see, no, no, he is at the top of his class in all subjects, especially brilliant in English and mathematics. But his behaviour….' he paused, not sure how to go on.

'Is he fighting? Have you been fighting with anyone, Nimesh? Not talking in class, I hope?' That was Baba, his father.

'No, no, it is nothing like that. Nimesh is a very well behaved boy. He is an example to others.'

'Then?' Ma and Baba looked and sounded puzzled.

'How do I put it – he does not seem to play with anyone. He does not like to play with the boys, I mean. He skips by himself or sits and knits! Knits, if you please! He even approached some girls to play with them, but naturally, they did not let him. He makes dresses for dolls!'

The principal fished around in a drawer in his desk, his bald head shining in the light of the lone bulb hanging down from the ceiling. He took out from the drawer a piece of knitting in mixed colours. He shook it in front of Nimesh's mother. Ma took it and recognised it as something she had started for her son. She saw that it had taken the shape of a doll's dress.

She thought quickly.

'Oh, this must be the one he has been knitting for his sister's doll. He loves her very much, you see. But I will ask him not to bring it to school if it bothers others. We will have a chat with him, don't worry Mr. Tarapore. Thank you for calling us.'

As they got up to go, Mr. Tarapore asked curiously, 'Don't you think that there is something odd in his behaviour though? I would suggest that you should take Nimesh to a doctor.'

'A doctor?' asked Ma in surprise. Baba nudged Ma, and she said, 'Yes, yes, we will make an appointment, thank you,' and nearly marched out of the door, angry and upset.

That evening, after tea, Baba signalled Ma with his eyes and promptly retired into his little study. There he immersed himself in his newspaper, leaving Ma to talk to Nimesh, as usual leaving all the unpleasant or confrontational tasks to her. He probably nurtured a faint hope that if he distanced himself from the problem, it would go away.

Ma did nothing other than to advise Nimesh to go play with the boys and do his knitting at home.

By then, though, the boys in school would not include him in their games, sensing that there was something different about this odd boy. Because Nimesh was extremely clever and topped his class every year, the teachers did not, or pretended not, to notice his oddness.

Matters, however, became worse as soon as Nimesh entered his teens. Many of the boys had started drawing breasts and parts of the female anatomy on the walls of the toilet and leering at the girls. They discussed this or that girl's breasts and how they had tried having or had already had sex. They discussed some of the female teachers as well. All this disgusted Nimesh. He helped two of the girls in his class with their math once a week, and he was constantly being asked by the boys whether he had done 'it' with them. They were two of the prettiest girls in his class, Asha and Lata. When he admitted angrily that he hadn't, they had laughed and remarked,

'You a bloody hijra or what?'

Nimesh had always known that he was meant to be a girl, that he was trapped in a man's body, that he was living a lie. He had been playing along with the unreality that was his existence because of his parents' position in their farcical society, and because he dared not imagine a life that did not really exist for people like him.

****

CHAPTER 29

Dadi

Two things happened that summer that changed everything. Nimesh's Dadi came to live with them. Lata made a pass at him.

The jeers and taunts were becoming worse at school. Even neighbours whose children went to school with him looked at him oddly. If he turned around suddenly, he would catch them laughing or looking disgustedly at him. The memory of it all still had the power to hurt Nimesha even now.

His only release was through his writing. He could not speak to his mother or father about the teasing at school because he feared the explanations more than he wanted their comforting. He also feared that their interference would make matters worse for him. Most of all, he wanted to protect his mother from any sadness that he knew she would feel if she discovered the truth about him. So he spoke to no one about his suffering and only let free rein to his feelings through his poems. The tight knot that formed in his heart throughout the day, caused by the cruel comments of his schoolmates, would find a modicum of release at night as he wrote. It was while signing his name to one of his poems that he thought how easy it was to become a girl simply by affixing the letter 'a' to his name.

'If only it was so simple to become a real one!' he thought.

It was while he was sitting at his desk writing one evening, when Dadi walked in. He had just written Nimesha, but as soon as he saw Dadi, he crossed off the 'a' at the end. Fortunately, Dadi could not read English but he still stuffed the poem in a blue cloth bag with mirror worked embroidery on it, as she came close.

She decided to organise his cupboard at that moment.

'How messy your things are,' she remarked. 'But boys will be boys,' she smiled with pride. Dadi had been very pleased that her first grandchild had been a boy. She always spoilt him rotten when she visited them or when Nimesh visited her during his school holidays. She just barely acknowledged the existence of Rene. In her view, Rene was just a girl, a temporary member of their family, to be looked after till she was married off to *her* family. Her grandmother only tolerated Rene because she had been born after Nimesh. She gave more pocket money to Nimesh and substantially more expensive presents to him as well. Dadi was very proud of the trophies that he won year after year for his excellent results at school. She spoke of him with pride to the neighbours, over the fence separating their front yards, knowing full well that their child was near to the bottom of *his* class.

Dadi had already mapped out his career for Nimesh. He would join the army just like his grandfather. She would choose his bride for him at the appropriate time. She had come to Delhi to live with them so that she could oversee his future and make sure that his mother Deepa did not influence him to choose some other profession.

Dadi let out a shriek that pierced the stillness of the summer evening.

'What is *this*?' She was holding out a dress, rather ugly looking, dark brown with a cheap tinsel border.

Nimesh turned white, but said as calmly as he could, 'It is a frock, must be Rene's.'

'Rene's? How can it be hers? It is so big!' Dadi exclaimed. She thought for a moment, a puzzled frown on her face. Then her brow cleared. 'Must be Mana's. Must have come in with our clothes. Or she must have sneaked it in amongst our clothes for washing. The cheek of that ayah!'

With that, she walked out with the offending dress and Nimesh let out the breath he had been holding, mentally kicking himself and deciding to be careful in the future.

****

The next day was Saturday, the day he went to Lata's house to help her and his other classmate, Asha. The first thing he noticed was that Lata was looking very pretty, in what looked like a party dress. He smiled when he saw she had even put on lipstick.

'Are you going out? Are we not doing any studies today, Lata? You look very nice by the way.'

It was spoken more like one girl to another, but Lata basked in the compliment, thinking how jealous Asha would be if she knew.

'Where's Asha?' asked Nimesh. The house was curiously silent as they headed off to the study room. 'I don't see Aunty or Uncle?' he added.

'Asha isn't coming today. Papa and mamma have gone to pick something for a present. Let's start before they come,' said Lata impatiently, and dragged him quickly into the study.

Little did Nimesh realise what Lata meant to start. As soon as he sat down, she locked the door and when he asked her why, she gave him what she thought was a coy smile, learnt from a Bollywood film, no doubt, and sat down on his lap.

'What are you doing, Lata?' asked Nimesh in panic. She put her lips on his instead of answering and, moving a little, quickly undid the zip of his pants and began to stroke him. For a stricken moment, Nimesh did nothing. Maybe subconsciously he had thought that this would be the revealing moment, that he may yet be a real boy.

But nothing happened to him. He didn't feel any excitement, his organ did not react, and it lay limp as ever. He jumped off the chair and, as he did so, Lata fell to the floor with her dress riding up, showing her pretty panties. Nimesh shouted,

'Now I know why no one is here! You have no shame behaving this way. I never imagined you would do this kind of thing. I cannot, I mean will not, behave in such a sneaky, sordid way. You should have more respect for yourself as a girl.' Nimesh was furious – at her because of what she had done. Although why he was angry at himself, he could not say. It was his last comment that infuriated Lata.

'I *have* respect for myself as a girl. At least I *am* a girl. What are you? Bloody hijra! Your organ did not even react! You look like a proper, normal boy but you are a nothing, a shell of a man. Respect my foot! Get out of my house, you nothing!' she shouted back, running to the door and flinging it open, her face red. As he went out, she slammed the door. He hesitated for a moment when he heard her loud sobs, but turned and walked towards the park to calm down.

Nimesh walked fast, hurrying to escape the demons in his head. Finding himself in the park, he ran on the track inside, not hearing or seeing anything. He was oblivious to the young trees so enthusiastically planted by his parents and the other residents when he had been just a toddler. The birds could have been dead for all he cared. Something seemed to die in him that day. He could not hide from himself or from anyone else that he was different, that he was a woman in a man's body. Lata would not keep quiet. Her rage at him and his insulting remarks would see to that. People would laugh at him all the more.

When his legs ached and he could stand no more, he went home. He walked straight to the bathroom, opened his pants and slapped himself till he blacked out. His father found him on the floor, and thinking that he had fainted while urinating, half carried and half dragged him to his bed. His mother, worried and anxious, sat by him all night and kept checking to see if he was breathing, even after the doctor had declared that nothing seemed to be wrong with him. He would have been shocked if he had seen the injuries Nimesh had inflicted on himself. Nimesh felt a rush of love for his mother and his only regret was that she would not escape being hurt when she learnt the truth about her son.

****

CHAPTER 30

Moment of Truth

If Dadi had not been the interfering busybody that she was, Nimesh would have been able to keep his secret longer. Being indifferent to Rene and with not much love to spare for her daughter in law, she spent most of her time pestering her son with complaints about his wife or pottering around in Nimesh's room. She insisted on organising his school bag even though he had asked her not to, and one day discovered a lipstick in a side pocket. Nimesh said that he needed it for a play at school. She found his knitting, and she lectured him on how boys did not knit. This was added to the list of boys did not cry, play with dolls, have long hair or take part in conversations with females, especially mothers. All this made them sissies.

One evening, everyone went to a wedding. Nimesh did not go because he had a test the next day. He had finished studying and had had his dinner, which the servant had heated for him. Then, seeing that he had the house to himself, he got a saree, petticoat and blouse from his mother's room and going to his room, put on his favourite film songs. Then dressing in his mother's clothes, he started dancing. He was an excellent dancer, his movements delicate and face alive with the expression of the particular mood he was portraying. The eye pencil and lipstick gave definition to the strikingly beautiful eyes and lips that he had inherited from Nani, his mother's mother.

The door opened just as he struck a pose, one hand outstretched gracefully and his body slowly twirling towards the door. At first, neither moved. Dadi could not recognise her grandson at the first instance. Nimesh was too shocked to move, his white face looking like that of a wax figure with his black kohl lined eyes and red lips in startling contrast. *What was Dadi doing back home?* They were not supposed to be back for an hour, at least!

He looked stupidly at his outstretched hand and broke the spell, saying,

'Dadi?' his voice coming out like a croak.

'It is you, Nimesh. What is this happening here? What are you doing?'

Nimesh whispered 'Drama...' and could not go on.

'Drama? Drama! I know now who has been doing drama all this time. Her voice had risen an octave. I was going to slap that woman at the wedding party. She was telling me that someone was saying all sorts of horrible things about you to her daughter. She was pretending to be angry and sympathetic, but I know she was not at all sorry from the inside. Saying something was *wrong* with you. Not a normal boy. Like a *ladki*, a girl, she said scornfully. I was so angry I could have hit her,' she said again.

'That is why I made Naren bring me back home. And what is this I see?' Her voice rose further. 'She was right! All those people have been laughing behind our backs because of this shameless boy. A boy!' Dadi continued scornfully.

Nimesh was miserably aware that by this time his parents and little sister were standing behind Dadi, all staring horrifically at him. All except Rene, who was staring with scared eyes at her grandmother.

'Drama! Yes, it is a drama all right! You have truly been play acting all this time! Playing the role of a boy. When all this time you have been, been...' Here her voice broke. 'What dreams I had seen for you! That you will be a man like your Dada! Join the army! The army hah! The army does not take effeminate creatures like *you*!' she ranted on.

Ma's voice interjected, 'Please let me talk to him.'

Dadi rounded on her. 'Talk to him? You? It is because of *you* that he has become like this! You and your mother. Your father is no man, he has no say,' she said irrelevantly. 'Buying him dolls, letting him knit. Knit, hey Bhagwan! Tying him to your saree. See what he has become, then! Wearing *your* saree. How could you produce such a child from your womb? You *must* have committed some terrible sin in your past life!'

She marched up to him and looked at his blouse and, putting her hand inside, pulled out two scarves that he had stuffed inside to look like breasts. 'See, see? Chi! Chi! What have you become? Is this *your* son?' she turned to Baba.

'Dadi,' said Nimesh finally, not being able to bear his mother's misery. '*I* have chosen to do this. This is who I am. Don't blame my mother for this. She did not know anything. It is *my* choice.'

She raised her hand in fury, more because he had defended his mother than because of what he had said about himself. She stopped just as Rene screamed with fright and ran and wrapped her arms around her brother. It was then that Dadi screamed the words that Rene was to hear later in her nightmares. Dadi dropped her hand but screamed,

'*Your* choice? Your choice! You are talking a lot, I see. Who are you? You are not a boy. Not a girl, certainly. You are a hijra. A hijra, hijra, hijra,' she screamed hysterically till Baba finally pulled her from the room and took her away. 'Close the door and change,' he said to Nimesh as he left. To his wife, nodding towards Rene, he said, 'I think she has seen and heard enough. Please put her to bed.'

His mother gave a last imploring look at her son and took Rene with her.

In the early hours of the morning following that tumultuous night, a slight figure in a girl's clothes, the head wrapped in a maroon coloured shawl, could be seen leaving stealthily from the back door of their house, if anyone happened to look out. At four o'clock in the morning, there was not much chance of that, as Nimesh had rightly judged.

He had not taken much with him. He was carrying the contents of his clay piggy bank in his pocket and his school backpack. This last contained two sets of his clothes, a sweater, a notebook, and some pencils. He had taken one picture in its frame, his mother's.

It was the memory of his mother's face as she tried to protect him from his grandmother's anger that kept him going, that had made him decide to run away in the first place, and that would in future prevent him from turning back whenever the hardships that he would face in life, tempted him to return.

Nimesh had realised that night that there were too many things at stake here. His father, Nimesh knew, could never stand up to his grandmother. He could not because of many reasons. His mother had always been a dominating wife and mother, and he had never been able to defy her or disobey her. There was the 'respect your elders' indoctrination from his childhood, which meant that even if he thought that his mother was clearly in the wrong, he was not allowed to say it. He was also too weak to take a stand and live a life faced with unpleasantness of any kind. In all these years, he had never been able to protect his wife from his mother's acid tongue and now things could only get worse.

Nimesh knew that between the domination and bigotry of one and the weakness of the other, his mother would be the one to suffer, and that was something he could not bear. He loved his mother, adored her unselfishly, and the thought of her suffering on account of him was one that he could not face. So he left, like a thief, in the early hours of that morning, never to return.

****

CHAPTER 31

Bittersweet

To seema@gmail.com; helen@hotmail.com

Subject Hi from Mumbai

Dearest buddies,

Thanks girls, for calling and for helping me to keep a clear head through all this. I do so miss you both. Jai has been marvellous as usual and has made it possible to meet Nimesha, organising different venues. She refuses to meet me in cafes or restaurants after the first time at a café. When in the middle of our meal, she had nudged me and had asked me to look around at the other people dining there, I was amazed to see everyone at the café staring openly at her and me. Not only that, there was a small crowd at the door when we walked out, one of them pointing and staring and saying what was apparently extremely vulgar, according to her, aimed at me.

'I am used to endless demeaning taunts hurled at me nearly every day, but I'm damned if I will tolerate any directed at you,' she declared. She's asked me to meet her in places where few people would be about on week days. So, Jai has organised meetings at, of all places, temple yards, a church, near the seaside, even a nursery. On the weekend, we plan to meet at a theme park! Should be fun, though.

I haven't felt so devastated even at my parents' passing away. My heart feels heavy, burdened as it is with guilt. It's been so hard for me to listen to the pain in Nimesha's heart rending story. Listening has been so devastating for me; can you imagine what she has gone through, experiencing them for real? I don't know which feeling fights for supremacy in my heart. Anger at the injustice of it all, frustration at the narrow, bigoted attitudes, or sadness at the treatment she has had to endure. My tears are always lining the edges of my eyes, threatening to fall at any time. I feel also a terrible guilt at having had all the love and advantages of a family, while she has had nothing but suffering. And for what reason? Because she was different, because she could not help what she wanted to be, what she is?

Her journey from the time she left home that terrible night until now, has been anything but story like. Nimesh's first encounter with kinnars was when I was born. He had seen the group who had come to dance and sing and had identified with them immediately. When mum sent him to give them money and clothes, he had casually asked where they lived.

'Why do you want to know? You like me?' had asked one of them lewdly, whispering in his ear. A few years later, some two years before that fateful night when he had run away, our next-door neighbour had a son born in the family. They had seven daughters in their wait for a son and there was much joy and celebration. Within days of the birth, a group of kinnars came to bless the baby. The group was large, expecting more from the parents, sensing that this time the new parents would be very generous.

One of the kinnars was very tall, and after the singing and dancing had finished, she saw Nimesh peeking over the fence. She stared at him very hard, as if sensing a kindred spirit. She ambled over to him and asked,

'Are you one of us?' At Nimesh's scared look, she laughed and said, 'If you need us, night or day, come to us, even if you are not one of us,' and laughed heartily at her own joke. She said her name was Sumati.

Nimesh did eventually find his way to the dhera, a house to which that very kinnar belonged, but stayed there for only three weeks. It was a community house called a *gharana*, where Sumati was the *nayak*, the head of the kinnar family. She took a strong liking to Nimesh and looked after him very well. However, one day, my mother had found the house after waiting outside the houses of three other gharanas, some of which were little more than slum dwellings. She had been sitting outside for three days in a row at different times in our blue car with the driver, sometimes driving herself, waiting to see if she could see Nimesh come or go. One or more of those times she must have taken me with her, which is what I recalled in my visions. Nimesh saw the car with his mother in it one of those times. Feeling cornered and desperate, Nimesh decided to leave New Delhi.

Sumati was sad to see him go, but before he went, she performed his initiation ceremony. This was a very elaborate event, necessary for him to officially become a kinnar. It is something like a christening ceremony, and is known as a *reet*, which he was required to undergo in order to become accepted as one of them. It all feels so surreal! Nimesha's guru, who undertook to train her for her life ahead as a kinnar performed the rites. Sumati explained to her new disciple the rules and regulations during the ceremony. They ranged from things like how a kinnar must walk, how she should serve water to someone. For example, a kinnar must not hold the glass at the top or the middle. She must balance it on her palms, held flat together. She explained also that her sari's free end should touch no one as she walked! A kinnar should never wear a guru's clothes, take the gharana's or the guru's name, nor ever sleep or lie down with her feet facing the guru! Back chatting to the guru or nayak was strictly forbidden. And many more! I can tell you, my brain has been getting dizzy with all this! But – to get back to Nimesha's heart-breaking journey….

Sumati, who could not read and write, dictated a note to the nayak, the head of one of the gharanas in Benaras, which explained also why she was letting go of Nimesha. Nimesha was disguised as a Sikh boy and with a plastic lunch box containing chapatti, potato curry and pickle for the journey, Sumati's husband saw her off, on a train to Benaras, now known as Varanasi.

So much for now. I am going to visit Nimesha soon in her office and spend as much time as I can to get to know her. I am also finally getting a chance to do some sightseeing in Bombay, now called Mumbai! Lots of city names have been changed recently, it appears! Girls, I have to finish now. Jai will be here any minute and he is going back to Delhi the day after tomorrow.

Bye for now, love you lots, Rene

****

CHAPTER 32

Following Nimesha

To seema@gmail.com; helen@hotmail.com

Subject Following Nimesha

My dear favourite people,

Today I went to see Nimesha in the 'office' that she works in. It is really a very makeshift arrangement, sub-let to Nimesha's 'family' by the owner of a convenience store next to the office. A part of the pavement has been encroached upon to create a space for a desk, where one of her chelas sits to take down names, problems, issues, incidents and so on – from kinnars waiting in a long queue that stretches for at least a kilometre down the street. The 'roof' is a blue tarpaulin sheet tethered to bamboo poles dug into the ground and supported by bricks stacked on either side.

Beyond this is the one room office occupied by Nimesha. She sits behind a desk piled with papers and used cups of tea. They are not really cups but small, narrow, transparent glasses, the kind you get in the dollar shops. A little boy takes them away from time to time in a wire tray with a handle that has six holes just large enough to hold the glasses in. Throughout the day, he serves tea to all the people who sit there for more than five minutes.

Nimesha is quite a different person as she listens and talks to the various people who come to her with their problems. With some, she is quite offhand and gets rid of them in five minutes or less. Chotu, as the tea boy is called, would grin and wink at me and gesture by moving his palm from side to side, as if to say, no tea. Later, when the last of her clients had left, Nimesha said,

'These are the regulars who just come to waste my time, and will not abide by my suggestions, creating their own problems. Some of them come only because they are annoyed at getting less money than they had expected from some new parent or from a wedding. They pester me to round up some kinnars to go badger those people.

When I don't agree to this kind of harassment, they just come here to annoy me instead.'

Today, Nimesha was wearing the salmon pink saree that I gave her, instead of her normal salwar kameez. She finds a saree less convenient, she says, especially when travelling on public transport, which is every day. She only wears them for special occasions now, such as a meeting with a government or other official, a special celebration, or the wedding of one of her chelas. Yes, they do get married sometimes, you know. But that's another story. You really can't tell by looking at her that she was born a boy. The way she talks to her clients is also different. The hand gestures, the facial expressions are exaggerated to appear more feminine, although not as much as some others. I wish they would talk and act normally instead of this caricatured version of feminine behaviour. It feels both sad and sometimes grotesque. Nimesha is different with me, though, much more understated and natural.

It is sad and sometimes downright horrifying to listen to the many hardships faced by the kinnars. Some problems that they bring to her seem hopeless. The causes and issues that she takes up seem so insurmountable to me. When I asked Nimesha what prompted her to establish her support group, she said,

'Someone has to do it. The hardships I faced, every one of us faces, for simple, ordinary fundamental rights are unimaginable for normal people, more so for you who have mostly lived overseas. I was a bright student but I could not get admission to school after I ran away. Rashmi arranged for me to take private tuitions till class twelve and I gave the examination only by paying a hefty bribe. But college was another story. I dressed as a male and used my given name to gain admission to study law in another city. But living in the hostel became impossible after some time.

Somehow, a few of the boys in the hostel came to guess the way I was and made life a living hell for me. Among other things, they wanted me to, you know, have physical relations with them. So, I ran away. After a year, I re-enrolled in a night college here and completed my degree.'

At my naïve 'Why can't you work at a regular job with all your qualifications,' her gaze grew bitter and for a minute she looked at me as if I was from some other world.

'Oh Tarini, nobody gives jobs to people like us. Even supposing one of us gets a regular job, other people will make life hell for us. That and the problems faced every day by the kinnars made me decide to form this group. We have to change society's attitude towards us and work hard to get basic social and human rights. In other places and states too some like me have formed similar support groups. My knowledge of law is useful to them too and we meet at least once a year now,' she said.

Nimesha has come a long way from that day when she had run away from home at night. In her words,

'There is so much untapped potential and intelligence among the young in our community. They can study and achieve anything if they can be provided with separate transgender hostels just like there are for girls and boys. At least then they would be protected from the insults and mental torture many go through and give up studying altogether. You can't have any conception of the numbers that are driven to suicide every year, Rene! Recently we have filed a petition with the state government to introduce such hostels, at the very least.

What shocks me most, sister, is the way *doctors* react. If we get past the initial hurdle of getting someone to see us, the lack of knowledge about us amongst the medical profession is baffling. They fear us; they have so many misconceptions about us. Do we have or not have sexual organs, whether they are female or male organs. Nothing prepares them for the reality, the shock they get. We are not even considered a necessary part of the medical curriculum. And for so many of us, the issues are psychological, which they just don't get. Depression and other mental health problems like suicidal tendencies amongst us are really not understood. The number of deaths by suicide is frightening, and are growing every day.

Even when we convince the person to see a doctor, registration is a nightmare because they want identification documents and proof of address. All kinnars do not possess such proof and in the absence of these documents, registration isn't possible. There is so much to be done and so much to fight for, Rene. Sometimes I fear whether I will see any results in *my* lifetime! But I still have to carry on, hoping and praying.'

'Did you miss home, our parents?' I asked her later when we were packing up for the day, but I was very afraid of her answer.

'Did I not!' sighed Nimesha heavily. 'It was all so frightening and strange! It terrified me that I would be caught. I was scared of being alone, insecure, hungry. Although Sumati guru was kind, she was not my mother whom I loved most in the world. It was unnerving at first to have a guru instead of a mother, to be a chela instead of a child. I missed my mother, especially when I was sick. I missed my home, studies, food, and proper clothes. Many times, I wanted to run away – back to the only home I had known, but I knew I could never do so. But over time the strangeness and the homesickness faded, mainly because of Sumati guru and Rashmiguru's kindness. I was lucky in that way.'

'Oh, I almost forgot. Sumati was very concerned about what had become of you. She asked me to let her know if I ever found you. I think, though, that it would be better if you wrote to her. I have her address on my mobile, here,' I remembered to tell her.

'Yes, I will. I owe her a lot. As well as to Rashmiguru in Varanasi and Ramaguru in Mumbai. The cold weather and lack of proper nourishment in Varanasi was making me sick. Ma had looked after me too well. I had no resistance to any bug that came my way. I almost died of pneumonia one time. For a long time, I was too weak to work. Rashmiguru allowed me to do the housework, keep the accounts till I got well. As soon as I felt well enough, I moved to Mumbai, where it wasn't cold.

In Mumbai, since I was a very good singer and dancer and better looking than some of the other kinnars, I was popular at the badhai performances at weddings, births, house warmings, etcetera. Somehow, I managed to keep out of prostitution. I recovered my health in Mumbai. My new mother Ramaguru realised my ability with math and my thirst for learning. After some time, she allowed me to take night classes to finish graduation. I started keeping accounts for the family. In time I started studying law privately and got my degree. Look at the coincidence, you and me being lawyers, although in such totally disparate circumstances!

Soon, though, the plight of the kinnars started encroaching into my consciousness. The preponderance of AIDS-related deaths, mental issues, suicides, the absence of basic medical care, not to mention rape, police brutality towards us, murder and diseases and lack of nutritious food was more than I could bear!

That was the time I met Manoj, my friend who is a compounder at a hospital. With his encouragement and help, I started this support group. I am now wanting to expand this into an NGO, but there are many roadblocks ahead on this path. However, I am in talks with some like-minded members of my community in some of the southern states, who have already achieved much more for the kinnars than us here in the west.'

When I hear what Nimesha has been through, my heart aches and I sometimes wish that I had let things be. But I also know that I couldn't have done that. I wonder how I am ever going to be the person that I was again. My life has certainly turned on its head. I so want to help with some of this, but don't know how to go about it.

Missing you guys. Wish you could be here with me.

Love, Rene

****

CHAPTER 33

Show Stopper

Jai called Rene one evening from Delhi to say in an amused voice,

'I think our man Sandy is smitten by the feisty Miss Naina. I don't think he has a hope in hell though. She seems to have a massive chip on her shoulder according to him.'

'I think it's a little too soon after her break up with Rohit; she's probably still feeling vulnerable although she doesn't like to show it. Ask lover boy to slow down,' advised Rene.

'Mmm, does that work for you too, Miss Rene? I'll make a note of it. Ah well, at least Naina's agreed to discuss what her NGO is all about with him. So, his charm has not all gone to waste, methinks.'

Rene also had exciting news for him. Nimesha had told her about a kinnar fashion show being planned at a national level. It was to be held in Mumbai and Nimesha had been selected not only to take part as a model, but to represent the Mumbai Chapter in the national organising committee.

'Nimesha is thrilled to bits! She feels honoured that they have chosen her to represent the kinnars here in Mumbai. It also means a hell lot of work in addition to what she's already doing, though,' Rene informed Jai.

'And?'

'How did you know there's an 'and'?' Rene laughed. 'Yes, I am going to extend my stay till then, of course. I can be of some help to her, hopefully. Well, I am so not going to miss this!'

'Keep me in the loop with the organising, Rene. I'd like to help in any way I can,' Jai offered.

The next few days went in a flurry of communicating with the organisers, meetings with members of the media, endless cups of tea and auditioning of the would be kinnar models. Rene took charge of the paperwork and emails. She had no clue about modelling but was not really surprised to learn that Nimesha did.

Jai, true to his word, helped with his contacts in the media and, together with Nimesha, Manoj and Rene, attended the media conferences.

Sandy used his contacts with an ex-girlfriend to hire a fashion show choreographer and, with the help of Naina and her fledgling NGO, took responsibility for organising the clothes and the rehearsals.

Naina moved to and from Delhi and Mumbai. Being in close association with Sandy, she soon realised that he was not just about flashing his money but that he was genuinely interested in what she and her NGO were doing. She found she couldn't have discovered a worthier cause for her NGO than helping to further the interests of the kinnars. She made up her mind during the weeks she spent helping to create a new platform for the kinnars, to show that they were humans like anyone else, that they could do what males and females could. Her NGO would represent them in Delhi, she decided.

Nimesha was in her element. She had finally got to do something fun, taking her mind off the problems she dealt with every day. She was blessed with an innate sense of style, which showed in the way she chose the clothes, whether they were western wear, sarees or other Indian dresses. She conferred with the choreographer, surprising the woman with some of her creative suggestions, who readily and gladly incorporated some of them.

Two days before the event was to take place, there was a protest march organised by some people who were against 'such a shameless show conducted by incongruous and vulgar beggars, who should not even be seen on the streets, let alone on a stage'. Nimesha was very worried and feared that the protest would turn violent. But with the intervention of Uncle Rajan and Jai's dad it was managed without too much trouble. In the end, it caused only a slight hiccup.

The fashion show was a tremendous success. Rene enjoyed herself and was proud to be so closely associated with the show's organisation, as were Jai, Sandy and Naina. Uncle Rajan and Shweta came from Delhi and to Rene's amazement, Sudha came too. But the real surprise guests were Nani and Nana from Kasauli. Jai had quietly arranged their trip and had kept it a secret from Rene.

The show stopper was, without a doubt, Nimesha. She looked magnificent in both her Indian and Western outfits and was a natural model, graceful and beautiful. The tears in Rene's eyes reflected those in Nani's as they watched her sashay up and down the ramp. They stood and clapped proudly as she thanked the audience, media and sponsors for their support. Suddenly, at the end of her speech, she saw Nani in the audience and froze for a second, not believing her eyes. She left the stage and ran to where Nani was standing and hugged her tightly, tears flowing down her cheeks. She remembered suddenly to touch Nani's and Nana's feet, as her parents had taught her to do years ago. Jai herded them all to the side of the hall, where they continued to cry and laugh at the same time.

****

To seema@gmail.com; helen@hotmail.com

Subject Reunions

Dearest besties,

What a show it was! To tell you the truth, I was anxious about the turnout, but I needn't have been. The media coverage and the curiosity among people about an unusual fashion show like this made sure that the tickets were sold out almost a week before the show!

It was all very emotional witnessing Nimesha's reunion with Nani and Nana. After the show, all of us went back to our hotel, taking Nimesha with us. It was a strange reunion. Nani and Nimesha sat close together, with tears escaping from their eyes every so often. They spoke in low whispers, with Nimesha's hands clasped tightly in Nani's. Aunt Sudha stared wide eyed from near the door and, although I don't think she is likely to acknowledge Nimesha to her kitty party buddies, she had the grace to say a few words to Nimesha. Uncle Rajan simply did not know how to deal with the situation. He blessed her when she touched his feet, mumbled a bless you, and stayed quiet after that. Shweta, as usual, had plenty of questions and caused the atmosphere to become a little lighter.

It's been a long and emotional day. I will get back next week after sorting out some bank and passport issues for Nimesha. Hopefully, she will be able to visit me soon. Meanwhile, I can't wait to see you guys!

Love, Rene

****

CHAPTER 34

Breasts are Important

Uncle Rajan, Aunt Sudha and Shweta left after a day as Shweta had her school term starting in two days. Sandy and Naina stayed back to finalise the plans and funding for Naina's NGO in Delhi. Jai looked on wickedly at Sandy as they made these plans and, after announcing with an exaggerated sigh that some people had work to do, he went to book his flight to Hong Kong, where he was needed for a few days.

Nimesha agreed to stay with Rene at her hotel for a couple of days. In truth, it thrilled her to spend some uninterrupted time with her sister. Living in such unusual luxury was a bonus. She touched the soft white towels to her face and bounced on the beautiful brass bed with its luxurious sheets. She picked up the many toiletries, smelt each one and asked ingenuously,

'Do you think I could take some of these, Rene? Rene felt a lump rise in her throat to see her sister taking such pleasure at things she had always taken for granted.

Rene offered to make tea in the little kitchenette in the suite, feeling happy and strange to be sharing a room with her sister, just as they had done as children, when they did not have separate rooms.

'Please no, I'll make my own. I still haven't got used to your dip-dip tea,' pleaded Nimesha.

'And I can't drink yours. Everything boiled together – tea, milk, water till you can't get the taste of anything at all. You're just like dad. He used to make it exactly like that!' exclaimed Rene.

As they lay on their twin beds one night, Rene asked,

'What's next? What's your biggest dream?'

'My biggest dream?' Nimesha thought for a second. 'To have basic human rights and to be accepted by the rest of society for who we are, is the biggest dream I have. To move from our peripheral existence to the centre of our own lives and have our identity recognised as separate from men or women. Rene, I have only just started dreaming now. The reality is a long way away.

We have had some successes, of course. We can now vote and we have the Adhar card, which is an identity card. But in reality, we have no identity still. We have paid a price for living in seclusion as we do, but then beggars can't be choosers. I want to educate all kinnars on their rights and also change some of *their* attitudes too. I want society to understand that yes, there are those among us that are black sheep who steal and kidnap and bring us a bad name, but that they are only a small percentage of our community. Just like there are similar people among the rest of society.

I want to change these attitudes. Fight for the fundamental rights of kinnars. Not to be laughed at, abused or feared.'

'But what about your personal dreams? You know, like love, relationships...?'

Nimesha smiled. 'These *are* my personal aspirations too, intertwined as they are with my very existence. But I do have one very personal wish that someday....,' Nimesha stopped and continued shyly, without looking at Rene, 'I am trying to save up for a hormonal treatment, you know, for real breasts, not socks stuffed into my blouse.' She spoke in a rush, a little embarrassed.

Rene was not at all embarrassed but was seriously practical, to Nimesha's surprise.

'Doesn't it cost a lot of money, though? As far as I can tell, you don't have any medical insurance,' said Rene.

'That's a fact, but one day I'll get there.' She named a figure and grinned as Rene's eyebrows shot up in her head. 'I can dress like a woman, look like a woman, but without breasts, I can't feel like a complete woman. Breasts are important, the most personal dream any of us kinnars can have. There you have it, my personal dream.'

Rene didn't have to think.

'I think I may have the solution. I will transfer the funds to you once I get back to Sydney and sort out a few things. It may take a few weeks, though.'

Nimesha looked shocked.

'Are you crazy? I can never let you do that! You too have a whole life ahead of you, and that's an enormous sum! No, no. I will not have you spending your earnings on this. I will not even hear about it,' exclaimed Nimesha, as she got up from her bed to leave the room.

Rene laughed.

'Hang on! It's not that. Aha! You also have the mistaken idea that everyone who lives overseas is loaded. I can't afford an apartment without a loan in Sydney, let alone have that kind of money sitting around. Dad was a shrewd investor, you know. He had done well for himself financially. The initial years in Australia were a tremendous struggle. He was forced into doing temping work while having to give some very difficult exams, even though he was a qualified doctor from India. But after he was admitted as a specialist, there was no looking back. We didn't spend a great deal on traveling. We spent most of our holidays in Australia and the overseas ones were in New Zealand or Fiji. Not yearly trips to India, as did most other families we knew. So, we have a house and a couple of investment properties all paid off. In addition, he had invested in a lot of shares. Those alone are worth a lot of money.

So, my dearest sister, you must agree for me to sell or rent the properties and give you half of what we get. After all, they are as much yours as mine.'

'Please do not sell the house. That won't do at all, no. The sale of one apartment should be more than enough for my needs. It will be of immense help to me; I will not lie. I can use it to buy a flat for myself with that and be free from paying rent forever,' replied Nimesha.

'In that case, I will also transfer your share of the rent from the house to your account, as well as whatever we get from the sale of the shares. Oh, I almost forgot! Among the things that I found in the suitcase, I found this.' Rene held it out to Nimesha, whose face wreathed in tears as she looked at it.

'What is it?' exclaimed Rene.

'It is a bank account in my name. Papa must have started it before he left for Australia. And look at the last entry. It is for the month before you said he died! Do you know what this means to me? It's more than what I need for my hormone treatment and probably even for my breast reconstruction. He must have thought about me after all, even though he could not protect me from his mother. Even though he did not know whether he would ever find me.'

'Did *you* never want to see us? Didn't you ever think of coming back?' Rene asked.

'On so many occasions, I've lost count. Nearly every night, I cried with Ma's picture under my pillow. I wondered about you, how you must have grown. I even learnt to forgive Papa for not having the courage to support me. But I was frightened of being rejected, of ruining your future, your chances of marriage and horrifying my family still more; so, I stayed away.

One day, when I was about seventeen years old, I took the night train from Varanasi with no conscious plan in my head and got off at the New Delhi railway station. It was afternoon when I found myself in front of our old house in Safdarjung Enclave. It was summer and most people who were home were resting or napping. I sat under the shade of a mango tree across the street, hidden from view, pretending to read a magazine, waiting for someone to come out.

In a little while, a car stopped in front of our house and a small girl opened the car door. She glanced at me and then walked towards the front door, while the driver took her school bag along with a bag of groceries and followed her.

For a minute there, I thought it was you until I realised you couldn't be that little anymore! At that moment, a young woman, who I think was the girl's mother, opened the front door, and the girl and driver walked in. I sat there wondering what to do and when the driver came back and drove away, I hastened to the door and rang the bell. When the woman came out, I said,

"Namaste behenji. I was looking for a lady, Mrs. Ray Choudhary, who used to live here. She was once very helpful and kind to me and I wanted to meet her."

"Oh, you mean Deepa didi and her family! The one with the young girl, yes? They left just a few years ago for Australia. I mean they immigrated. In fact, we bought this house from them just a month before they left. So sorry I can't help you but I can try to get their address if you wanted to write."

"No, no, that is all right; don't worry about it, thank you for your kindness."

She just smiled; it was obvious to me that she hadn't realised who I was. Otherwise, she probably wouldn't have been so kind.

'So you knew we were not in India anymore?' asked Rene.

'Yes, I knew. I went back feeling sick and hopeless. In some corner of my heart, I had cherished the thought, however unreal, that I would be able to see all of you again. Maybe even share some happy times together. One of my chelas, Ragini, has done that, you know. I am so happy for her. Her happiness gives me a kind of vicarious satisfaction. As if it were *my* family I was meeting. I have always wondered whether Ma ever thought of me, the way I did, every day,' answered Nimesha sadly.

'I am sure she thought of you every single day. My guess is Ma died of a broken heart. I used to hear her cry at night when she thought I was asleep. And it's obvious from the mementoes in the suitcase and the bank account that Dad never forgot you either,' said Rene earnestly.

Nimesha cried as Rene finished speaking and the two hugged each other, sitting with their arms around each other for a long time.

****

It took a few days of navigating the tedious and annoying red tape to sort out and activate the account which Nimesha's father had maintained for her so far. Jai came to the rescue because he, as usual, knew somebody who knew somebody in the bank who could fix the problem. The Indian system of *jugad*, a clever, perhaps irregular arrangement or an expedient solution, never ceased to amaze Rene. Nimesha on her own would never have been able to access the money.

It was the same when she applied for her passport. An 'official' birth certificate needed to be made, based on the original hospital certificate. But that identified Nimesha as a boy. Uncle Rajan's network became useful here, in sorting the confusion in the gender identity, after much more of the jugad and a considerable amount of money to grease the hierarchical palms. Much of the governmental red tape was circumvented in India in this way.

In the week before she returned to Sydney, Rene divided her time between Nimesha and Jai. She knew Nimesha would be able to visit her in Sydney in about four or five months, but she did not know when she would to see Jai next, if at all. That thought depressed her and, much as she tried to quash it, it just would not go away.

She tried not to look at him at the airport and took a long time over her farewell to Nimesha. She quickly bid goodbye to Jai and walked with rapid steps towards the check in window, desperately trying to hide her tears.

****

CHAPTER 35

Seema's Sangeet

Nimesha danced as if possessed. And possessed she was! With happiness and an exhilarating sense of freedom. For the first time in her life, she was dancing with abandon, without shame, without the fear that Dadi or anyone would come upon her doing something forbidden. She felt free, unfettered. She was not dancing at a wedding for the money, nor was anyone being forced to watch her. They were watching because they wanted to. She loved the beautiful clothes she wore, the attention she got and the genuine appreciation she received from the onlookers.

Anyone could see that Nimesha was, in essence, an artist. Her dance movements were perfect, fluid, and only a very trained eye would notice that she was not a professional dancer. She was lost in the emotion of the moment. Her eyes shone; her feet spun. She was at once Radha; she was Meera; she was a sultry eyed seductress, and she was a coy heroine. The bells on her feet rang with the expression of her feet. The last piece was choreographed by her for herself and Rene. As they danced in the traditional Kathak style, Nimesha's passion burst forth in her dizzying turns and flashing eyes. When the two sisters made the final turns with their skirts swirling gracefully, syncronising their turns with the rhythmic beats of the music, Nimesha could not remember when she had been so happy.

Suddenly, the music changed and Nimesha surprised and delighted all the guests with a spectacular Flamenco piece, in which Nick's mum joined her at the end.

Several guests surrounded them and hugged her, many full of praise for her dancing. Rene's heart swelled with pride and her happiness reflected Nimesha's. *If only she could convince Nimesha to stay with her!*

In that fleeting moment, Nimesha too wished likewise. She was so happy. But she knew she would never be truly happy unless her life meant something to her beyond this everyday enjoyment. There was too much at stake. True, the kind of acceptance she had with Rene and her friends, she would probably never experience in her life back home. The joy she had felt exploring Sydney with Rene and her friends, her feeling of complete anonymity, thrilled her. No one looked at her twice, disgustedly or otherwise, except maybe to admire her looks.

****

Nimesha went to the Sydney Mardi Gras festival and the magnitude and freedom of being able to celebrate being different that she witnessed stunned her. She loved the music, the colour, the pageantry, the costumes. Most of all, she loved that men were holding hands with men, that women were kissing women openly, and that transgenders of all shapes and colour were strutting around the parade and on the floats with pride.

However, to strive for a moderately decent existence away from life's periphery was her aim now. For others like her, if not for herself. If it took her entire life trying to secure the basic facilities which others took for granted, she would spend it so trying. Too many lives depended on her work as an activist. She could not, did not want to change her life's course now, much as she could not stop breathing.

At least, there was this beautiful light in her life now. She had found her little sister! She was grateful for her love, her support. Rene had told her that all that her parents had left to her was equally Nimesha's. She thought happily that she could use the money to buy her own little apartment. She guessed that Rene was being more than generous, but her sister had waved off her protests saying that nothing would compensate Nimesha for the years of misery that she had gone through. Nimesha thought with wonder of Rene's kindness. So many siblings, rich though they may be, would have ended their relationships if there was money or property in question.

Rene tried very hard to persuade her sister to stay with her in Sydney.

'Why do you have to go? Why can't you stay here with me? I don't want to lose you now, having found you after so many years,' said Rene beseechingly. 'Even my friends here like you so much already. And there is so much you could do here. You could live a life of dignity, of acceptance here, you *know* that,' Rene implored, trying to make Nimesha change her mind, although she knew in her heart that it was next to impossible.

Nimesha placed her hands on Rene's shoulders. 'Yes, I know. And more than anything, it would mean that I would have *you* near me. However, much as I would love to stay close to you, I can't, Rene dear,' answered Nimesha sadly, seeing her sister's woebegone face.

'And think of the benefits to you. You don't have to worry about anything. I will sponsor you. You are my only living family member, so immigration should not be a problem,' Rene continued as if she hadn't heard.

'But what will I do here Rene? Work at a Woolworths checkout? Even if I could study and became a lawyer here like you, of what use would it be to my work back home? The work that I do in Mumbai is very important to me, for all of us. At the moment, I am involved at the local, state and national level too. I would never be happy knowing I did not do what I could have for many of my sister kinnars, who are far worse off than I ever was.' Nimesha's face was full of the bittersweet regret she was feeling at having to reject her sister's pleas.

'I need to think of the others who depend on me. And what of Monica, Ragini, my other chelas? They look to me for guidance, for support. We have taken some, albeit baby steps towards forming an NGO to try to solve some of our problems. I gave them hope, something to strive towards. They will feel completely abandoned without my presence, my moral support. You know how hard we have struggled to get even this far. All of that pain, struggle, my run-ins with the bigots in the bureaucracy, our efforts to achieve a modicum of decency in our lives would fall down the cracks if I am not physically there. It is so easy to lose heart and hope. We've been kicked around in the past and have faced so much despair. I can't just abandon either my other sisters or all that effort. Please understand. I don't know what, if anything, we can achieve through this NGO, maybe nothing really significant. But I would spend every day here feeling guilty and thinking about what I could have done if I hadn't thought only about myself.'

'I am sorry Nimesha, to be putting so much pressure on you to stay. I realise I am being selfish. This NGO, how are you going to find funds for it?'

'That is another ball game entirely,' laughed Nimesha. 'We have one company who has agreed to support us, but it's a very small venture and the amount pledged will barely even meet our initial set up cost. And I refuse to take monetary help from Jai bhaisaab and Sandy bhaisaab, although they offered to invest. Both of them, along with Naina, are already helping in ways that I thought I would never see in this life. Which is why I need to start full on efforts to get funding that will take care of equipment, phone, computers and rent, which is a big issue in Mumbai.'

Rene let out an impatient sound. 'Really! And you never thought of discussing it with me, right? I spoke to you while in India about our parent's house in Kirribilli, which was left to me and is currently on rent. It's a very high value property. What I plan to do is to sell it and give you that amount. I should be able to organise that in a few weeks. It's the best solution. You could meet a fairly sizeable chunk of those expenses from that,' she said, smiling excitedly.

'Are you crazy? I will never let you do that. It's yours. You have already offered me more than enough already.'

'No Nimesha. It is equally yours. It belonged to our parents. You could use it to buy your own apartment in Mumbai and use part of it as the office of the NGO. At least, you will not have to keep paying the rent. It will get you way more than by selling the apartment here.'

'It would take such a great load off my mind and would solve my biggest problem of office space. But I can't take all of it. We will go equal shares,' stated Nimesha firmly.

'Half won't get you a shack in Mumbai, you know that. Moreover,' Rene put her arms around Nimesha as she said this. 'I have got so much more from our parents that you never did. The education, money, support that I took for granted should have been yours too. I can't take away your past pain, your suffering, your loneliness. I can't give you back your childhood and erase the hurt and despair that you went through. At least let me do this, please,' she begged.

Nimesha's tears were flowing freely as Rene finished speaking. She hugged Rene in acceptance of her offer, saying, 'Hush now. I have you. That is enough to wipe away the pain of the years past.'

In the end, she had to accept that Nimesha's determination and her decision to go back to Mumbai was one that she must live with. Rene had to admire her for her commitment to travel such a long and arduous road and vowed to support her in any way that she could.

****

CHAPTER 36

A Visitor

Helen rang the bell and walked in, her arms weighed down with shopping bags.

'The things I do for people!' she grumbled at no one in particular, as Rene let her in. 'Hey Nimmi, see what I got you. I had to go to the Asian supermarket for these ugly looking *saag*. I forgot what it's called, some choy or the other. Hubby tells me it is a weed eaten by indigenous Australians and used by specialist cooks, if you please! Well, it's all yours to do with as you like, hon, ugh!' she announced dramatically.

'Good evening and hello to you too,' Rene said sarcastically. Where's Seema?

'Oh, she's bringing up the rest of the stuff after she finds parking, that is. What's wrong with her? The door's open for Chrissake!' she added as the doorbell rang yet again. She marched off to the door and came back looking somewhat subdued, along with Seema. She was unsuccessful at hiding her gleaming eyes and signalled Seema to come to the kitchen.

'Some handsome hunk asking for you,' Seema told Rene nonchalantly. 'It's good I am getting married in a few days, otherwise he would be in serious danger from moi.' She winked at Nimesha, who had run curiously to the door and had come back, looking like the cat who'd got the cream.

'Who is it?' Rene asked as she went to the door and stopped short. She could have sworn later that she had stopped breathing for some minutes. There was Jai, looking as handsome as ever. No, handsomer; and she felt a hunger of a different kind gnawing at her. His eyes were not laughing as usual, but reflecting that hunger. The 'how... what are you doing here' died on her lips and instead his 'God, how I've missed you' sent her into his arms. She felt as if she had come home. Rene felt she would be crushed; his arms were so tight around her. He kissed her with the passion born out of the long separation and Rene didn't want him to stop, for once wishing that they had been alone.

'Have you missed me?' she asked him, knowing as she did so how lame it sounded.

'Missed you? You've got to be kidding. I have been sick with longing to hold you like this. I have been going slowly mad at work, wondering when I could just take time off, or better still, leave it all to my brother and run away,' he laughed. As he bent towards her again, Helen's voice said from behind,

'Do you think you two lovebirds can let me by? See you in um, let's see, an hour?' She looked at them and went to get the remaining bags from the car, laughing. As soon as she was back, she unceremoniously dropped the bags that she was holding and hurried to confer with the other two in the kitchen.

'Hey listen, you two, can you believe this? The surprise visitor is the famous Jai! I just saw them melting into each other! That secretive Rene! She gave us no clue that things between them had progressed this far. I think guys we should leave them alone asap. Isn't he gorgeous?' she said, rolling her eyes and keeping her voice as low as she could.

'I am not going right away. First of all, we had planned this dinner ages ago for Nimmi here and I want to see what Jai is like. Suss him out, you know! Come, Helen. But I tell you what, let's buzz off straight after dinner and leave the lovebirds to themselves. If you like, you can come over to our flat, Nimmi,' offered Seema.

'And be a gooseberry there instead? No, thank you. My room is quite far from Rene's and I am pretty used to being invisible when I need to. Anyway, I am going to the Blue Mountains by the early morning train and after that I want to explore the Jenolan Caves on my own. So, you know, they can pretty much do their own thing,' smiled Nimesha.

'That's great, then,' grinned Helen. They got busy helping Nimmi as she made her greens and stuffed *parathas*. She was quick and neat and had dinner ready in half an hour with pakoras for entrée, a raita along with grilled eggplant, the cholai greens and stuffed bread.

As Nimmi took the fritters and green chutney made with lime juice, mint and coriander leaves, she stood with the tray in her hands over the coffee table, looking towards the door but not really seeing anything, a wistful look in her eyes.

Helen took the tray from her hands and went with her to the kitchen to get some dinner plates and cutlery.

'What's the matter Nimmi? Are you homesick or something?' she asked.

Nimesha, who had very fair skin, actually blushed.

'Out with it!' exclaimed Helen. 'Who is he? Or she?'

Nimesha, all flustered and embarrassed, finally babbled, 'There's nothing definite. He is a compounder at the hospital where we send some of our girls for treatment, that's all.'

'Mmm, that doesn't seem to be all, I can tell, hun. Out with it.' Helen, when she got the bit between her teeth, was not one to let go that easily.

'I like him!' Nimesha burst out. His name is Manoj. He has always been very helpful and understanding while liaising between the hospital and our people. He actually *gets* our health issues. At least he treats us like humans. He has been helpful with his contacts with some doctors, who agree to see us and treat us. Most of them don't even know how to treat us. I have been taking his help whenever we've run into any problems. Most of the other staff pretend we don't exist, will not give us beds or even treatment. They give us the least priority, but not him.'

'So, how does he feel about you?' pursued Helen.

'I don't know. He is kind to me. He calls me on the phone sometimes, but mostly to talk about the situation of one of our girls in the hospital,' Nimesha replied.

'Why don't you ask him?' was Seema's suggestion.

Nimesha looked horrified. 'Oh my God, no. How can I even dream of doing that? It would be so presumptuous. I may even lose his friendship! That would be disastrous for our girls. And for me. We would lose the little help that we get as well. No, no, not in this life.' She looked up as Rene and Jai walked in and smiled at the happiness she saw on her sister's face.

'Arrey Jai bhaisaab, it is such a pleasant surprise to see you here,' she said. Jai surprised her by giving her a bear hug and she turned away to hide her tears at this gesture. Jai noticed but pretended not to and started chatting with all of them as if he had known them for years.

It amazed both Helen and Seema how much he remembered about them from what Rene had said to him so many months ago. They loved him instantly and Rene, who could read both of them like a book, could see them getting ready to plot, scheme, and pressure her to love him likewise.

As if she needed anyone to pressure her to love Jai. She knew today, if she had not known earlier, how impossible her life was going to be without him. She had been living in a state of limbo ever since her return from India. Only the presence of Nimesha in her life and her friends had made life worthwhile. But she did not know how Jai really felt, what he thought he would achieve by coming on a visit to Sydney. She could not see any future still, how a long-distance relationship could sustain itself. She had her work, her life here and he had his businesses so far across the world.

****

CHAPTER 37

Nimesha's Love Story

When Rene informed Helen and Seema about Nimesha's decision not to immigrate and their discussion, Seema said,

'And of course, there's this guy, right?'

'What guy?' Rene asked, surprised.

'The male nurse or compounder, she said. She said that there was nothing concrete yet, but that she has feelings for him. Helps her out a lot, it appears. We suggested she should ask him about how he felt, but she was shocked at the mere idea. Maybe you can talk to her,' added Helen.

That night, after dinner Rene went to Nimesha's room and, sitting on the chair next to the bed, asked her sister,

'So, what's this about a male nurse?'

'Oh, I should have guessed that those two would spill the beans!' Nimesha answered, trying to evade an answer.

'Uh huh, out with it. I want all the gory details, how you met him, what's going on, etcetera, etcetera,' Rene smiled, guessing Nimesha's intention.

'He's a compounder, actually, and doubles as a nurse when there are emergencies. I had gone with Sheila to the hospital. She had been badly beaten by the pimp who controlled the area in which she worked. They had refused to admit her, see her even. She came to me for help, so I went. We went to the emergency entrance but they asked us to wait. And wait. We kept getting fed with some pretext or the other for the delay.

When no one came for nearly three hours, I raised such hell, screaming at the staff and threatening to undress right there, that the male nurse who was on duty heard and came out to see what the hell was going on.

"Do you realise that this is a hospital? People come here for treatment and need their rest and quiet. And here you are making all this commotion. Do you have any sense of shame?" he yelled at me.

"And we, of course, are not people. Three hours! It takes three fucking hours to attend to an emergency patient? Or is that 'treatment' reserved for the likes of us? Or were you hoping that she would conveniently die, and matters would end there?" I had yelled back at him.

"No one informed us," the nurse had replied quietly, looking ashamed. "Stretcher! Bring her in quickly!" he had called out to two orderlies after taking one look at Sheila's condition.

His name is Manoj. After he had cleaned and treated her wounds and arranged for an X-Ray and got the doctor on duty to look at her, he came out to see me. He knew from Sheila's condition and her wounds that she had been beaten and asked whether I had filed a complaint with the police.

"You're kidding me, right? Most of those dogs are in cahoots with these pimps. Why make things more complicated for her and probably for the hospital, hmm?" I had replied.

"Oh, so you can yell here and threaten to dance naked, but you don't have enough guts to take it further. Emotion but no *jigar*, no courage. Here, this is the doctor's prescription for her medication. He is my friend, one of the few who will see patients like her."

"Well, why don't they? Are we not entitled to treatment just because we are kinnars? Or is the oath they take the hypocrite's oath?" I had mocked him.

"I can't answer for them," Manoj had replied. "Most of them have a lot of misconceptions about hijras. They are quite clueless about their anatomy, even. Do they have any sexual organs? If so, which kind, male or female? They don't teach this in medical schools, you know. Which they should, as the doctors are in for a rude shock otherwise. So, they lack knowledge, which they need to be able to treat the hijras correctly. And the nurses and other healthcare workers show even more discrimination because of their ignorance and superstitions. Anyway, think about what I said about going to the police and get Sheila to rest for a few days, now. Also, if you need help, this is my number on the envelope," he said. Nimesha paused in her narrative, reminiscing.

That was the first time someone in the medical profession had treated one of her kind like any other patient in Nimesha's experience. What he had said to her, had preyed on her mind long after that day and had sowed the idea of doing more for her community, to find solutions to their plight. Getting the right to health care became her first priority.

'After that, I kept running into him during some of my visits, accompanying one or the other of my chelas. Whenever he was on duty, of course,' continued Nimesha.

'Initially, we met only at the hospital and I phoned him sometimes to make sure he would be there to attend to a chela, but later I went and met him to have tea at the hospital café during his break, to discuss how we could better the situation of our lot. From there we talked about our stories, and mine seemed to fascinate him so much that he could never seem to have enough of hearing about it again and again. He would stare at me when he thought I wasn't looking,' Nimesha said, smiling.

One day, she had deliberately caught him at it and asked boldly, 'Why do you stare at me so much? It's quite rude and makes me very uncomfortable.'

Manoj had been startled enough to burst out, 'Because you are exceptionally beautiful! I mean, no one can tell by looking at you that you are anything but a woman. You could easily give Aishwarya Rai a run for her money in the looks department, you know!' He had stopped, aghast at himself and looked terribly embarrassed. Nimesha had burst into a peal of laughter at such a generous compliment, but had secretly been very flattered.

'Your looks could be a tremendous advantage if you wanted to get into Bollywood,' Manoj suggested.

Nimesha laughed at his credulity. 'Are you serious? How naïve can you be? For all my looks, I am still a kinnar and no one will ever consider the likes of us in any 'normal' role. And I wouldn't fit the Bollywood hijra stereotype either.'

'Well then, what about if you started an organisation to deal with the problems that you face every day? You've been talking about it for the last few months. Isn't it time to put money where your mouth is? And your looks will surely make things easier? At least to get a foot in the door,' Manoj suggested, little realising how she would construe his ideas.

Nimesha had grown red in the face and she rounded on him, her eyes flashing with anger.

'How dare you even make this suggestion? You think all of us are ready to sell ourselves, whether it is for money or favours. And you think all of this is so easy because *you've* had it easy all of your life. I just have to sashay into a bureaucrat's or minister's office with my proposal, taking with me my beautiful face and no money; and they would beg to come to the inauguration of my, this organisation, right?

Let me inform you, Mr. Manoj, beauty is a curse for outsiders like us unless we have our birth families' support. All I would achieve is to come to some fat politician's attention. I know; because I have had a lot of attention in the past from the likes of these. It doesn't matter whether they are straight, gay, heterosexuals, sometimes the women too. After that, life would be more of a hell than it already is, and who would come to my help then? You? To stitch up my wounds or maybe call the morgue?' Still simmering with anger, Nimesha had stood up as she said this and slammed down some money on the café table for the tea that had gone cold.

Manoj had stood up too, the shock written on his face palpable. 'No, no, no, no, hey Bhagawan, that is not what I meant at all, not even remotely. I should have thought what it would sound like, but all I meant is that, in this world, being presentable just helps, but I am sorry I even suggested it. And no, I have never thought that it was going to be a cakewalk to travel on this difficult path, of challenging so much discrimination, especially for hijras. It's bad enough for transgenders and gays. But you can be sure that whatever you decide and whenever you decide to take that road, I will be there walking with you,' he said in a rush.

'Why?' Nimesha had asked.

'Because from where I am, I can see that special something in you that has courage, understanding and empathy that can take this forward, not to mention your qualifications as a lawyer. And you are wrong when you say that my life has been easy. Yes, perhaps not as difficult as yours, but hard all the same,' Manoj said quietly.

'He told me then that he was gay but hadn't had the courage to come out. One of the night nurses had suspected as much when she had tried to seduce him and he hadn't responded. He was afraid that if people knew, not only his colleagues but his patients would avoid him.' Nimesha told Rene.

'Manoj has been instrumental in getting help for so many from our community in so many ways. So many suffer from mental health problems like depression and suicidal tendencies. A doctor needs to get what drives them towards a state of such helplessness. We have no one to depend on apart from our community. If our birth families abandon us and we have no children or earnings, who do we turn to? What is there to look forward to, Rene?' Nimesha paused, as if looking at some far off place that Rene couldn't see.

'We have a long way to go before medical staff can be more sensitized, society more helpful. I wish.... I wish parents could understand the needs of children like us and that bureaucrats would do more than talk. That is why I feel I am racing against time. So many problems, so little time in one life to achieve all this. At least, though I can try to start something which others like me can continue, I hope,' she sighed wistfully.

****

CHAPTER 38

Will She?

Seema's wedding had all the elements of a big fat wedding and it was interesting to see the similarities between the Indians and the Greek sides of the couple. They all laughed, talked and sang loudly, even spat on each other to ward off the evil eye that dared to park its gaze on the happy couple. They had an Indian wedding and a ceremony at their church, followed by a reception at a vineyard in Hunter Valley. Jai and Nimesha were invited too and everyone there had a marvellous time.

On their return from Hunter Valley, Jai sat in the lounge and made a Skype call to Sandy. After bringing Jai up to date on their business matters, Sandy asked,

'So, what's going on with your love life? I am reading the signs right, right? I am sure of it!' He had that 'cat that had swallowed the cream look' and brought his chair closer to his laptop, leaning forward, peering closely at Jai's exasperated face.

'Ooh, how the mighty have fallen! The great 'touch me not' Jai is in love! No help for you now, man.' He ducked a long distanced cuff on the ear from Jai and laughed out loud.

'Seriously though, have you told her?' At Jai's expressive look, he sighed. 'You'd better do that soonish bro. Someone else might snap her up if you don't hurry and get your act together. I don't mind being in the running, come to think of it.' he grinned.

Jai gave him 'the big bro look' as Sandeep called it. 'To tell you the truth, Sandy, I'm scared of asking her,' sighed Jai. 'We live so far away from each other. Rene has her life in Australia, her friends, her work, all that she's familiar with. Her friends here are as good as her family. I know how traumatic their move was when she was a child and how bewildered she has been with all these revelations in her family. How can I ask her to uproot herself again, even if she feels the same as I do?' he asked.

'How serious are you about her? I mean, is it the real thing?' Sandy prodded.

'I love her, idiot. I feel horrified mooning about her like this, but really, I don't think I can live without that damned woman! There. I've said it.'

'Then *do* something about it. You know I've got your back with the business in India. While you're there, you could explore business options in Australia and possibilities for managing our off-shore operations from Sydney.'

Jai walked thoughtfully towards the kitchen to make himself a cup of coffee. He knew what he had to do.

****

Jai made some enquiries and a few days later, looking for Rene, he found her loading the dishwasher. He watched amusedly as Rene methodically placed the knives alternately with the spoons in the dishwasher. He had watched her before, but now realised that she actually followed a system while he, if he ever needed to use the one in his home in India, would keep them haphazardly in any slot whatsoever. Rene shooed him away when he tried to help and said,

'If you really want to be useful, stay away from the dishwasher. You can dry the ones I've taken out, thanks.

'I can always take care of the cooking while I'm here. Or forever, if you like,' replied Jai. He was looking around the room, trying hard to look nonchalant as he said this. He hadn't realised that Helen and Nimesha had come in as he was speaking and now saw them glance at each other with suppressed excitement. Jai put on a mock scowl and nodded his head to shoo them away. The two of them retraced their footsteps with great reluctance.

'Forever?' Rene asked, a bit dazedly. She was uncertain whether she had heard right or what he could mean, if she had.

Jai forgot the little speech he had tried to prepare. Instead, he said in a rush, 'Yes, forever. I tried saying to myself that it wouldn't work, that I would have to forget about any long term relationship with you. But I can't stay away from you, Rene. What I am trying to say in my own clumsy way is that I can't live without you, my dearest Rene.' He held her hand and pulled her after him into the family room.

'You've got under my skin, babe,' he said, his eyes serious. Gone was his droll manner. 'I love you, Rene. A lot. Clichés be damned, I really can't live without you.' Jai held out his hands and pulled her into his arms as he said this. He smiled self-deprecatingly and said, 'Rene, please end my torture and say you'll marry me.'

It took Rene a few seconds to collect her wits and to try and clamp down the feeling of dizziness flooding through her whole body. She gave herself up to burrowing even closer into Jai's arms before pulling away a little and saying dazedly,

'But how is it going to work, Jai? You in India and me here?' she asked.

Helen's voice came from outside the door. 'If you don't say yes first and right now, you'll have Nimesha and me to answer to.' The two of them had been listening unashamedly through a crack in the doorway.

Both of them grinned and rolled their eyes and Jai went soundlessly to shut the door. 'Can't have any privacy with you two around,' he told them.

'Is that a yes?' asked Jai when he returned, his voice strained and hopeful. Rene smiled.

'I love you, Jai. More than I can say. There's nothing I want more than to marry you and spend my whole life with you. I just can't see how we're going to make this work, though,' Rene sighed, her worry showing.

Jai led her to the bright yellow window seat and sat there, pulling her down next to him. He said, 'I've been giving this a lot of thought, sweetheart. That is why I haven't dared to ask you before. Sandy, as you know, has been looking after the overseas offices in Hong Kong and Singapore for a few years now. He doesn't say it, but he misses home and it does get pretty lonely out there. Although both of us are close to mom, he's always been the baby of the family and especially attached to her. And now with dad being ill and mom feeling insecure, I feel he would be happier back home in India. In fact, when I was telling him about my worry about a long-distance relationship, he kind of suggested that if we swapped our work domains, that *could* solve our problem.' He paused as if thinking what to say next and continued, saying,

'I haven't worked out all the logistics and details yet. I didn't know, kind of still don't, what you were going to say. We've had some initial discussions to work out whether to move one of our offices or setting up a completely new branch here in Sydney, and so far, things are looking good. There are some immigration formalities and a bit of paperwork remaining. I have been given an indication that it will all be good to go in a few weeks, at least as far as approvals are concerned. Nick has been a great help and guide throughout.'

'Oh my God, you have been busy. No wonder you've been happy to be sightseeing all by yourself. And those long chats with Nick, not learning Greek, I presume?' Rene jumped up, only to place herself snugly on Jai's lap and kissing him. She was a very pleased young woman and thought she loved Jai even more now.

'God, woman, are you even going to say yes?' groaned Jai.

'Yes Jai, I will marry you,' said Rene smiling, and they spent the next few minutes smiling their joy and restricting themselves to kissing each other, knowing that the two curious women in the next room would not leave them alone for much longer.

True enough, when they opened the door, Helen almost fell in and her expression aimed at Rene asked the all-important question.

Rene hugged Nimesha and Helen and announced, 'It's a yes, of course!'

'It had to be!' said Helen smugly while Nimesha danced a little jig and hugged and kissed Rene repeatedly. She liked Jai immensely and was hoping for the two to get together for a long time. She hugged Jai, saying,

'Congratulations Jai, my brother. You are my brother now, aren't you?'

'Of course! Is there any doubt?' Saying this he twirled Nimesha around the room and picked her up for the last one. She shrieked and begged to be put down and collapsed on to the little white chaise lounge, giggling unabashedly.

Rene looked at Nimesha, and pangs of both happiness and nostalgia for the past ran through her heart. She wished her sister could be this happy and carefree forever. She still nurtured the hope that one day Nimesha would agree to move to Sydney, so that they could see each other often and make up for the lost time together.

The doorbell broke into her reverie, and Rene opened the door to a young boy carrying a white box and a bouquet of red roses. As soon as she closed the door it rang again and Seema made her appearance. She was on her way to their new apartment not too far from Rene's when Helen called to give her the news. Although she still needed to finish her packing before she left on their honeymoon the next day, she could not keep herself from being a part of her dear friend's happiness. She ran straight to Rene and hugged her tightly. It surprised Rene to see the tears glistening in Seema's eyes and when she questioned her with her own, Seema just said,

'Happy, happy.' She went and conferred in a whisper with Helen, who produced a beautiful cake in the white box while Seema fished out a bottle of champagne from her ubiquitous oversized bag. Jai and Rene burst out laughing.

'There was no way they were going to let you say no,' he told Rene. He addressed the rest, saying, 'Guys, we're going to select the ring. We'll see you in a bit.' Jai grinned wickedly, seeing the girls' disappointed faces. 'After the champagne and cake, of course,' he added, restoring the cheerful mood in the room.

****

After the champagne was drunk and the cake eaten, Jai took Rene to the City as Sydney's downtown was called. At the jewellers, Rene pushed away all the large stones and finally chose one with a small ruby surrounded by tiny diamonds. Jai pocketed the box, and they drove to McMahon's Point near the harbour. As they walked down the slope after parking the car, Jai asked her where she would like to go for dinner. Rene thought he was planning to give her the ring there.

Instead, Jai took her to one of the beautiful arched stone gateways in the park, just near the water. As soon as they reached the gateway, Jai got down on one knee. He drew Rene's hand in his, and smiling, asked her,

'Dearest Rene, will you marry me?' The harbour bridge, the Opera House in the distance and the deep green water of the harbour all became a blur for Rene. She had always made fun of romance novels and the soppy scenes as she had called them, and there she was, revelling in the most clichéd scene of all. Although the question had been asked and answered, she still loved that Jai could be so romantic. She could only nod at first and then her whispered yes had Jai taking out the ring with a flourish. As he placed it on her finger, Rene felt a rush of happiness. Jai stood up and held her close for what seemed ages. She hadn't realised that she had closed her eyes. A small burst of clapping had her eyes open and when she looked around, Rene saw that a few late afternoon strollers were looking at them curiously and smiling. A couple congratulated them and a few waved.

Jai and Rene had their dinner in the revolving restaurant in the Sydney Tower to celebrate their engagement, where the two planned to let his parents know first before making any formal plans.

****

The three of them travelled to Tasmania together, much against Nimesha's protests about being a third wheel. After they returned to Sydney, during the last two days before Jai returned to India, Nimesha took herself on walks along the cliffs at Watson's harbour and Bondi Beach, revelling in the freedom to be herself while giving Jai and Rene some time alone.

Two weeks before her visa was to expire, Nimesha received news that her application for an NGO status for their organisation had been brought forward for consideration and review, and that she would need to travel to Mumbai for a meeting scheduled for the week after. Much as Rene hated to see her leave even a day earlier than she had to, she understood what was at stake and how important this was to Nimesha.

****

CHAPTER 39

Raison De'etre

Immediately after her return to Mumbai, Nimesha was completely swallowed up with meetings, getting paperwork ready and trying to secure various approvals for her NGO. One evening, when Jai came to look her up on a business visit to Mumbai, he found her with her head in her hands, looking completely exhausted.

'Rene was right. She sensed you are having a rough time and not letting on. You can always discuss stuff with me, you know. I won't charge you,' he exclaimed.

'Who knows?' laughed Nimesha. But her mood immediately lightened the moment she saw him, which was usually the effect Jai had on most people.

'Come on, tell me all while I give you a neck massage,' Jai said and began gently kneading the tense muscles knotting in her neck and shoulders.

'Oh God, if you and my little sis were not getting married, and I wasn't so terribly in love with Manoj, I would marry you in a second,' she winked laughingly.

'You wish,' replied Jai with a grin. 'But seriously, what's up?' he asked.

Nimesha had been busy. She had been petitioning for a number of things, the closest to her heart being the right of the kinnars to adopt.

'I am so tired. We are fighting for houses to be given to us. The right to normal jobs. Do you know how many of us are forced into prostitution because nobody will give any of us a job? And because so many of us are sex workers, HIV and AIDS are rampant. We work with other NGOs for their treatment, but their workload is huge. We need one of our own! My chelas want me to fight in the elections! What good will that do? I am running pillar to post every day, but things barely move here!'

After listening to what Nimesha had had to deal with all by herself, Jai offered to help her with some resources.

'Look Nimmi, I came to see you not only because Rene was worried about you but because I have some suggestions that we could discuss – and then see how we could go forward. My experience in business and financial planning should be of some use and my legal department is at your disposal.' Jai invited her to his office for a meeting to complete the proposal.

****

On the following Monday, in the afternoon, Freny, who had accompanied Jai to Mumbai announced through the intercom,

'Jai, Nimesha is here to see you.'

As soon as Jai saw Nimesha, he knew something momentous had happened. Her face had an excited glow, and happiness radiated from her.

'Manoj has proposed,' she burst out happily, not noticing that Freny, who remained at the door, was listening unabashedly.

Jai came around the desk and hugged Nimesha, sharing her happiness. 'Congratulations Nimmi, I am so happy for you. When did this happen?'

'Just an hour ago, we were having lunch together, and he put this ring in the rice pudding, the idiot. I nearly swallowed it,' she laughed happily. After Freny had congratulated Nimesha, both she and Jai said together,

'We should let Rene know.'

Jai made the call and they could hear Rene's excited and happy squeals, drawing smiles from everyone in the room. In a few seconds she went into planning mode, announcing to Nimesha that she would organise everything.

'Hold your horses,' laughed Nimesha, 'we haven't even thought of when we're going to tie the knot yet, Choti.' Nimesha filled Rene in with all the details of Manoj's proposal and the two siblings chattered away, as sisters who are close to each other, do.

Jai called Manoj to congratulate him and the two decided to meet for dinner, as Nimesha was committed to a meeting with other kinnar representatives regarding the petition for their right to adopt.

****

Jai picked up Manoj from his hospital and after they had ordered their drinks and food, Jai asked curiously,

'How is it you have been at pains to hide the fact that you're gay from your work mates but have dived headlong into a rather more controversial step of getting married to a kinnar? How will you deal with all that attention? Don't get me wrong, it's admirable what you're doing.'

'They don't need to know. It's my life and I intend to keep it private. And it's not admirable. It's not some kind of social work. I love Nimesha.'

'Of course! And you're lucky. What about at the wedding though and later at your get-togethers? Won't they suspect? You would need to tell them at some point.'

'Oh, I see what you're thinking,' Manoj laughed. You think we meet socially, have drinks, dinner and all of that, like you perhaps do. But once I leave work, that part of our lives ceases to exist. At the hospital we work together, see pain and suffering together, but we don't *do* things together. Not socially anyway. Social events are usually enjoyed with their own kind and, by that I mean, the same class, community, family, maybe neighbours. Only once had I heard about an office picnic being planned by people belonging to the Kayastha caste. No one else was asked. You Jai *saab* belong to a different stratum of society. Forgive me for saying so. You are the upper class, where caste and sexual orientation does not matter that much.

You must know that hairdresser, the famous drag queen Sasha. Your class shows pride, an inverted snobbery even, in being friends with someone like her, being one of her exclusive group of clients. She's rich and famous. But you don't forsake class. What I'm trying to say is that there is not much chance of my work mates meeting us outside of work, let alone at my wedding.'

Jai laughed, 'Sasha? I go to my childhood barber in Khan Market still. Can't afford Sasha. What about your parents, family?'

'My parents live in Katra, a small village in Uttar Pradesh. I had wanted them to live here with me, but when they came here on a visit, the strangeness and crowds of a vast city like Mumbai got to them in a few days. They were so used to the quiet of the village, pottering about the garden, or sitting on a charpoy with friends in the evening, seeing neighbours, chatting with them over the fence; a place where everyone knew everyone. The fact that even neighbours did not know you made them lonely. With nothing much to do other than watch television, they were bored to death.

I visit them once a year, usually during the festival of Holi. We plan to have a simple wedding here in Mumbai, after which we will visit them and deal with the issue then. All I know is my parents love me and my sister very much and while they will be shocked at first, I am their only son and they will stand by us against the world, if the need arises,' sighed Manoj.

****

CHAPTER 40

Promises to Keep

'Meet Aneesha, my chela. She is one of the lucky ones, training to be a hairdresser,' Nimesha introduced, the pride unmistakable in her voice. She was getting her hair done by the said Aneesha, while Rene looked on with eyes glistening suspiciously. Nimesha was going to be a bride! They were in an upmarket parlour, frequented by Mumbai's rich and famous. It being Monday, the parlour was closed to customers, but the owner of the parlour had agreed to let Aneesha work that day.

'The owner of the parlour, Rishabh, is a friend from the time he had run away from his village with no place to stay. He was lying under the tarpaulin in front of our office and we had let him stay inside till he found a place. Now, so many years on, he has made quite a name for himself with the 'page three' types. His haircuts and styling and makeup skills, have made him very popular and much sought after, especially with the Bollywood and modelling crowd. He will do my make up later,' Nimesha continued.

'How did Aneesha get hired by him?' asked Rene.

'It was quite by chance. Aneesha was looking for training, and Rishabh happened to have four weddings to cater to and was faced with a sudden shortage of staff. The day she walked into his parlour was her lucky day. Rishabh hired her as general help, the only condition being that she came to work wearing jeans and the parlour tee. The rest is history, as they say. Aneesha is really very talented with hair and make-up and Rishabh noticed. Rishabh has hired her permanently, and she has finished her probation only last week,' Nimesha finished with a satisfied smile.

Nimesha, as everyone had known she would, was a beautiful bride. As Manoj and she had wanted, the ceremony was a simple one. Nimesha had said that anything more would distance her from her chelas. She refused any gift that would be of personal use to her, saying that if she got too comfortable in her life, she would lose her focus. Manoj and she had only agreed to accept help with the NGO in whichever way it was given. Uncle Rajan and Sudha, along with Naina and Shweta, arrived a day before the wedding, and with them came Nana and Nani. Manoj's sister was the lone representative from his family. Every one of Nimesha's chelas and a few kinnars from other dheras also attended the wedding, and for that one day they seemed to have forgotten their unfortunate existence; singing, dancing and drinking the night away. As she was leaving with Manoj for their short honeymoon in the nearby foothills of Matheran, Nimesha whispered to Rene,

'Look at them. They're so happy for me. I am so lucky, Rene. Most men will not marry a dark skinned woman in our society. And Manoj has married me. Me, a kinnar!' She blinked away the happy tears and Rene hugged her tightly.

Nimesha's NGO had taken shape during the previous three months and was finally inaugurated at the end of it. Her joy knew no bounds. She still could not believe that it had actually happened. She was overwhelmed by her wedding present from Jai, who had generously set up a trust fund for her NGO. Rene had arrived for the inauguration and had stayed for the wedding, little knowing that there was going to be another one shortly.

****

The call from the hospital came two days after the wedding. Jai's father became seriously ill, and the doctors were not sure how many days he had left. When Rene and Jai went to see him, however, he seemed his normal self and had taken the news that he had not long to live, with a quiet calmness. He expressed only one wish. That he wanted to see his son Jai married before he died. Jai did not know what to say.

'This wasn't the way I had wanted it to happen. How could he ask that of Rene?' he asked his mother.

His mother read her son's quandary and said to Rene, her hand on her shoulder,

'It's all right. He's just being sentimental. I'll talk to him, don't worry. You can decide on the date later.'

'What's to decide? Now's a good time as any. If Jai hasn't changed his mind and can organise whatever needs to be done, the sooner the better,' said Rene, taking the matter out of their hands.

So it was that the next day, Rene and Jai were married in a waiting room in a hospital in Delhi, with only their two families attending. Rene looked radiant in a beautiful pink saree given to her by Sudha. Jai, in a simple sherwani suit, could only look at his bride and wonder what he had done to deserve such an unselfish and beautiful woman in his life.

If anyone had told her even a few months ago that she would get married like this, she would have thought they had lost their mind. She hadn't really had any picture in her mind except the few ceremonies that she had been to in Sydney. All she felt now was worry for Jai and his family, now hers as well. Jai had told her they would have their 'normal' wedding and celebrations when they were ready, but all that was now secondary to the fact that they loved each other and had sealed that with this simple ceremony. That and the happiness she had seen on Jai's dad's face.

It was as if he was waiting to see his older son married, because in the early hours of the morning, Jai's father died in his sleep.

****

A few weeks after Rene's return to Sydney, she received an email from Nimesha, which made her very happy and excited for her sister. It went thus:

Dear Rene,

It has finally happened! I have the news that we have been waiting for, for so long. Kinnars have now been given the right to adopt! Even now I have to pinch myself to make myself believe that it has actually happened. Can it really be true, I say to myself. And guess what? Manoj and I haven't wasted any time. We have already sent in our application to adopt a child, a girl preferably. We are really busy now. Our NGO has started work with the hospitals and clinics to treat kinnars with AIDS and HIV. The craft training centre has teachers now for embroidery, block printing and Madhubani painting. My cup of happiness is nearly full, choti.

I am so happy that you and Jai have finally set the date for your wedding celebration in Australia. I am sorry that Manoj will not be able to go, but it is too soon after Diwali and they get overwhelmed with burn accident patients. But not for the world will I miss my baby sister's big day. Waiting to see you, your very own sister,

Nimesha

Rene could feel the joy emanating from Nimesha's words, and she revelled in her sister's achievements. Six months later, news came that her own cup of joy would soon be full. Jai rang to say that his visa had been approved and that they could look forward to having their 'proper' wedding in Sydney. Seema and Helen, who had been waiting impatiently, immediately launched into planning Rene's wedding ceremony and reception.

The wedding, which consisted of a celebrant formalising their Indian wedding, took place in a beautiful stone courtyard, set in the middle of one Sydney's lesser known heritage gardens, the steps from the courtyard leading down to the sea. Rene was dressed in a simple Indo Western gown in a delicate mauve, her hair piled high in a messy bun. After she and Jai had signed the register and she was dancing in his arms, Rene felt she had come home. Her gaze rested one by one on Nimesha, her grandparents, her two cousins, Sandy, her uncle and aunt, Jai's mother and her two dear friends. Not long ago, she had thought she had no family in the world and all at once, their loving presence surrounded her today.

****

Soon, too soon it seemed to Rene, the time came for Nimesha and the rest of their family members to return to India. Nimesha's flight was the last to leave. Rene and Jai were also leaving for their honeymoon to the Fiji Islands a little after, on the same day.

As they stood at the fork of the two corridors leading to their separate destinations, Nimesha and Rene hugged each other with mixed emotions. Their hearts were heavy knowing that they had to part, but the realization that each now had a sibling that they loved, and the ever present hope that they would see each other again, gave them the strength to choke back their tears. Nimesha walked away first, Rene watching till she could see her no more. Jai came then and, putting his arm around her, quietly led her to their own new journey.

As the plane taxied on the runway prior to taking off, Nimesha looked out at Botany Bay beyond the runway and thought about the long way she had come. From time immemorial, people in their society had been intolerant of those who did not conform to the larger idea of normal – those with different beliefs, sexual preferences or physical attributes. And she was dreaming of being accepted into mainstream society. She wondered if it was ever going to happen in her life or at all. She felt justifiably proud of what she and her organisation had achieved so far, but she also knew that they had miles to go before she could fulfil even some, if not all, the promises she had made to herself.

She took out the picture she had received just before she had come to Rene's wedding. And as she sat gazing in wonder at the picture of the baby girl that had been sent to her for their adoption, she hoped that the day would come when she and others like her would be able to live – not in the periphery of others' existence but be able to find a place among them.

****

THE END